LADY OF MADNESS & MOONLIGHT

Rogue Ethereal Series - Book 3

ANNIE ANDERSON

LADY of MADNESS & MOONLIGHT
Rogue Ethereal Book 3
International Bestselling Author
Annie Anderson

All rights reserved
Copyright © 2019 Annie Anderson
No part of this book may be reproduced, distributed, transmitted in any form or by any means, or stored in a database retrieval system without the prior written permission from the author. You must not circulate this book in any format. Thank you for respecting the rights of the author. This is a work of fiction. Names, characters, businesses, organizations, places, events, and incidents are either the products of the author's imagination or used in a fictitious manner. Any resemblance to actual persons, living or dead, or actual events is purely coincidental.

Edited by Angela Sanders
Cover Design by Danielle Fine

www.annieande.com

For my daughters.
May you always pull each other from the ashes.

"Monsters are real, and ghosts are real too. They live inside us, and sometimes, they win."

— STEPHEN KING

BOOKS BY ANNIE ANDERSON

GRAVE TALKER SERIES

Dead to Me

Dead & Gone

SOUL READER SERIES

Night Watch

Death Watch

ROGUE ETHEREAL SERIES

Woman of Blood & Bone

Daughter of Souls & Silence

Lady of Madness & Moonlight

Sister of Embers & Echoes

Priestess of Storms & Stone

Queen of Fate & Fire

PHOENIX RISING SERIES

(Formerly the Ashes to Ashes Series)

Flame Kissed

Death Kissed

Fate Kissed

Shade Kissed

Sight Kissed

SHELTER ME SERIES

Seeking Sanctuary

Reaching Refuge

CHAPTER ONE

For the hundredth time today, a fist was aimed at my head, rocketing toward me with enough power behind it to knock me into next week. That was, if it hit me, which considering the luck I had today, was entirely likely. Managing to duck the fist coming for my face at the last second, I scrambled to the side before swinging up and returning the favor, landing it in his not-so-soft middle. Honestly, it was like I was bare-knuckle punching a brick wall.

I only got to enjoy the pained "oof" for a second, though, because another fist or a leg or an elbow was coming, and if any of the above hit me, I'd be a mushy stain on the floor. My opponent was much better than me on every level—except for the magic one—but I cared too much about the opinion of his pack to fight dirty. Plus, he had a set of sharp fangs he could use to level the playing field at any moment.

A leg came out of nowhere and swept mine out from under me. I landed on a hip—the pain of the bone meeting mat knocking the breath out of me. But I learned early on that staying still was just about the worst thing I could do. Scrambling so I wasn't on the receiving end of the haymaker aimed my way, I managed to dodge another fist.

"I swear to the Fates, Marcus, if you let her get a black eye today of all days, I will hurt you in ways you can only dream about." Barrett's voice echoed through the gym.

A strangled wheeze made it past my lips which only pissed Barrett off more.

"And not in a good way," he added, the threat hanging in the air.

Barrett really was the nicest. I should send him a fruit basket or something.

Marcus, Barrett's mate, periodically took time out of his busy schedule to beat me into something more than the weak, combat-challenged hot mess I'd been for the last four hundred years. And when he thought I actually learned something, he set members of his pack loose on me while he critiqued my technique.

Kinda like right now.

Finnegan Lorenson was a beast of a man, and as his name suggested, practically a Viking. With his white-blond hair, bulging muscles, and can-do attitude, he was one of the larger men I'd fought today. Oh, and by "can-do," I meant more like a "I'm gonna fuck shit up and eat your entrails for breakfast" attitude. The majority of Marcus' pack were of the happy, family oriented, inclusive sort. Not all of them were wolves, not all of them were able to shift, but all of them were included, taught, and protected. It was what I would imagine the Weasley's would be like if they were a pack.

But not Finn.

He didn't like fighting me. Hell, it would be more accurate to say he was offended to be fighting someone like me. I couldn't figure out if it was because I was a woman, a witch, or because I was half-demon. Maybe it was all of the above. Either way, it didn't feel like Finn was sparring—or after that last hit, not anymore.

I ached everywhere, from the tips of my toes all the way up to my scalp, and I was about done with my "no magic" self-inflicted edict. There wasn't a way on this earth I could beat Finn without a little magical backup.

What happens if you can't use magic, Maxima? What are you gonna do then? Aidan's voice ran on an auto-loop in my head every single time I sparred. This used to be his job—teaching me how not to be a weakling—but I'd distanced myself from him over the last six months. I wanted to think it wasn't me being petty, but since his brother, Ian, kicked me to the curb, it was more than likely.

The rejection still stung, the pain of it fading slowly like the pink of a brand-new scar. It wasn't going away anytime soon, and the reminder would always be there. I wasn't the kind of woman he wanted. Those latent wraith traits of his made him need to protect the "little lady" when I was anything but. I didn't need for him to tell me what to do or how to do it. I didn't need him to protect me.

All I'd needed was a partner. And that was something he didn't know how to be.

Honestly, I wasn't sure I was the right woman for anyone, but damn if it wasn't lonely.

The musings over my joke of a love life stole my concentration, and I landed on the mat once again, the breath that I so desperately needed whooshing out of me in a single pained gust. But then Finn aimed a kick while I was still down, and I realized I'd had about enough.

Served me right for mentally whining over Ian.

Before his foot could connect, I wheezed out a command in Latin. *Subsisto.* Snapping my fingers, Finn froze, his foot reared back to strike, malice on his face. No, Finn wasn't playing at all.

Gingerly, I rolled away from his stationary foot before heaving my body to standing. The world spun for a second, but I managed not to upchuck or pass out. And then I noticed Finn's foot inching toward completion, my stopping spell barely holding him. No, that just wouldn't do.

Gathering myself, I decided to give the spell a little more *oomph*. Instead of snapping my fingers, I whispered my commands on the palms of my hands before stretching my arms wide and then brought my hands together. The clap that echoed through the room not only made Finn stop, it knocked him on his ass, his body sliding across the canvas from the momentum of it.

The pack of wolves on the risers watching Finn and I "spar" snickered like children as their packmate slid across the room like a big, blond hockey puck. I looked up just in time to see Barrett's face turn an alarming shade of crimson.

"It's not my fault she was holding back," Marcus grumbled, not expecting Barrett to hear him.

Barrett and Marcus held seats on the Ethereal Council. Barrett maintained the seat for all the witches in North America, and Marcus for all the shifters. When I first met them, I had no idea they'd already been mated for several centuries. Now that I knew, their bickering made so much more sense. It was even kind of cute.

They wanted me to take the demon seat, but I'd been on the fence about it. Until six months ago, I'd been a Rogue. Putting me in a seat of authority seemed to be a bigger leap than I was ready for.

"It's your fault if I say it's your fault," Barrett scolded his husband. "Spar means light touch to no touch, not tear each other to shreds."

Wolves could heal a hell of a lot faster than I could, so their definition of "sparring" was more along the lines of fighting for my life. And while I would heal, a black eye would put a cherry on the shit pie I was about to eat.

"Come on, Max. Wipe yourself up off that mat. You've got a big day ahead of you."

Barrett didn't have to remind me. I knew exactly what was in store for me later tonight. The presentation to the Fates. Only the "p" in presentation was a capital and came with a laundry list of rules and regulations that chafed against me like sandpaper.

I really hated rules. Especially when I had no choice but to obey them.

Groaning, I blew a wayward strand of blue hair from my face. Half my hair was falling out of the messy bun—messy meaning it took me thirty minutes to make that shit look cute—the sweaty tendrils plastered themselves against my neck and the side of my face like I'd glued them there. Which totally explained why Barrett gave me a bitchy tongue-cluck of derision.

"You had to pick a fight today of all days?"

Of course I did. If I was going to walk into a room full of Ethereal upper crust and let them look me over like a slab of beef, then I was getting all my rage out now. Really, it was safer for everyone that way.

"What? You don't think you can make me presentable in the twelve hours we have to get ready? Some fairy godmother you are."

Barrett's lips parted to answer me just as I felt a frisson of magic rake across my skin. I wasn't supposed to be able to feel magic being spent. I wasn't supposed to be able to see the motes and hex lines or catch the way each spell's scent differed from the other. I perceived all parts of magic —how it looked, how it smelled, how it felt. Everything.

The sensation of a wolf jumping to his other form had a very specific composition. It was part moonlight and part the breeze flowing through a thatch of trees. It was wildness and blood and freedom.

And death. Lots and lots of death.

It wasn't like in the movies where the human side of a wolf would bend and shape into another form, cracking bones and growing hair. No, that was movie magic and a load of crap. Real wolves were two parts of the same soul, fighting for dominance and dominion on which side of the Ethereal coin would fall. Or at least that was how Marcus explained it. Not that it made any sense or explained where the hell the human side went when the wolf appeared in a puff of magic smoke.

But that didn't matter much right now. All that really mattered was that there was a wolf in the room.

Not that it was technically a problem right this second, and not that it was my job to deal with it if it actually became a problem. Or at least that was what I told myself so I didn't start some shit in the Alpha's house. I wasn't in charge here, and as far as wolf politics went, I knew exactly dick. Yeah, I'd been fighting wolves all day, but that was at the Alpha's behest.

I knew without looking at Marcus that this phase was not sanctioned, and judging by his growl, it wasn't welcomed, either. I slid my gaze to Marcus, giving him a little head shake to signal I would handle it on my own. He grinned, likely remembering the time I nearly exploded the high court room with a snap of my fingers.

Turning slowly as to not agitate the apex predator, I surveyed the animal before me. Pure white fur from the tips of his ears to his toes made him seem cuddly at first, the texture soft and plush like a puppy. But letting my guard down even a little would be a huge mistake on my part.

Especially since this particular wolf was closer to three hundred pounds rather than two, and the top of his head probably reached my chin. Not that I'd let him get close enough to measure. Only one of Marcus' men had hair that color, or eyes that shade of ice. And only one I'd just knocked on his ass.

Finn.

I'd only managed to subdue him with a stasis spell that barely succeeded in holding his human form. Something told me that same spell wouldn't work so well on his wolf—if it worked at all. My only real hope here was if I didn't have to fight him in the first place. An evil smile stretched across my lips as it finally came to me.

"And who's a pretty puppy?" I used the exact same voice I'd use when I came across any old dog.

Denver was super dog friendly. They weren't allowed in my tattoo shop because of cross-contamination rules —but coffee shops, restaurants, and libraries? Puppers were everywhere. And while I shouldn't let my guard down for even a millisecond, teasing Finn seemed like the best course of action.

"Look at you all floofy and beautiful. You are a big old ball of gorgeous, aren't you?"

Hoots and hollers erupted from the risers along with a few belly laughs, signaling my cue to keep going despite Finn's vibrating growl.

"Now, Finn, are you going to bite my arms off if I pet you? Because that would be rude."

Finn's growl got louder as he showed me his teeth—razor-sharp canines dripping saliva.

"Finny-boy, if you don't play nice, you won't get a treat," I said in a singsong voice, breaking away from Marcus and Barrett and slowly circling back into the room in a wide arc.

I wasn't giving my back to this wolf, and I sure as hell wasn't letting Barrett take the brunt if Finn decided to charge me. Marcus would kill him for letting his wolf go free, and for some reason that seemed like a waste.

Finn's claws dug into the mat, ripping the plasticized fabric, yellowish mat innards spilling out around the sharp talons.

I opened my mouth to make another verbal jab, but old Finn wasn't having it. He charged, coming at me straight-on like a man instead of how a wolf would. Wolves were pack hunters: sneaky, skillful. Finn was all brute strength and zero finesse. He fought like a man in wolf's clothing rather than ceding to his animal.

He barreled toward me, refusing to heed Marcus' bellowed shout, ignoring his pack's yells to stop. But I knew better than to flinch.

Finn was playing chicken. I'd bet on it. Granted, I didn't want to be munched on by a three-hundred-pound wolf, but since my other option was to be presented like a show pony to the bougie Ethereal upper crust, it was really shit or diarrhea at this point. And while I couldn't help my galloping heart, or the flash fire of adrenaline racing across my skin, a part of my brain—the one with a little bit of a death wish—only whispered a single word.

Fun.

CHAPTER TWO

Planting my bare feet, I waited for Finn to leap—waited for him to strike—keeping my face a bored mask. I saw the exact second he realized I wasn't going to move. Alarm crossed his wolfy face as he skidded to a stop, the tips of his front paws barely millimeters from my bare toes.

"Trying to scare me, Finn? *Tsk, tsk, tsk.*" I clucked, assessing the magic of his wolf.

Motes of pale-blue magic danced around his head like an aura. It made me wonder if I could manipulate them.

"*Ipsum revelare*," I murmured sweetly, snapping my fingers. *Reveal yourself.*

It was a spell I'd used only a few times, and one that made my gut ache every time I used it. It reminded me of betrayal and a hurt that soured the triumph of staring a werewolf down and not flinching.

It reminded me that not everyone was my friend. Not everyone cared if I lived or died. Hell, some of them even thirsted for it. It reminded me that even the good guys could turn on you.

The ice-blue motes above the wolf's head roiled, darkening to midnight with threads of silver before he seemed to fade and melt into the shape of a man. I could feel the crowd around us react to me bringing a wolf back to his human form with a snap of my fingers.

I could feel their unease. Their panic. Witches weren't supposed to be able to do that—weren't supposed to be able to control a shifter's phase. But I wasn't all witch, and they needed to remember that.

"Do you know why I perform non-lethal spells, Finn?" Even to my ears, my voice sounded damn near dead.

I should be safe here in Marcus' home. I shouldn't have to defend myself or worry if some idiot will get a wild hair up his ass and attack me. All of the mirth of teasing, all the happiness crumbled to ash on my tongue.

I should have known better than to let my guard down. That was how I got hurt.

"No." Finn's voice was little more than a breath of

wind across my cheek as I stared *up, up, up* into his ice-blue eyes.

"It's because I consider you my friend, and I do my very best not to hurt my friends. Are you my friend, Finn?"

His eyes flitted to the side for a second as his nostrils flared, scenting me. Finn was the kind of handsome you'd only see in movies, a shock of white hair atop his tanned face. His icy eyes seemed to glow like stars. His full lips pulled into a smirking sort of smile, and I knew he wasn't as scared as he should have been.

None of them were.

And I already knew his answer—whatever it was going to be—was going to be a lie. Just like his sparring, Finn was dirty, shady. He was a cheat, and he liked inflicting pain. He would kick a man when he was down. And the more I looked into his eyes, the more I knew, he didn't just hate me for being a witch. He hated me because I was a woman, and I'd beaten him.

He was a small-minded misogynist and hated other Ethereals.

"No," I answered for him. "You're not, are you?"

What was likely a prank or a chance to poke fun at me incited an urge in my belly that I couldn't name. Maybe it was bloodlust, or maybe it was just a dire kind of need to make him pay. This was my demon side at work—the side that thirsted for something I couldn't pinpoint. Not blood. Not revenge.

Justice.

"Do you know what a demon does, Finn?"

He shook his head, the smirk falling off his face.

"They make people pay for their crimes. Unfortunately, it's after death, so there is no chance to learn from the mistakes you made. There is no chance to choose another path."

Finn's eyes widened just slightly, realizing too late that I wasn't just some woman he could push around. I wasn't the weak witch that sparred with his Alpha.

Turning my head, I met Barrett's eyes. "I'll take the job."

Barrett's mouth stretched into a sly grin, his blue eyes sparkling like I'd just given him the best birthday present ever. I'd been hounded for the last six months about taking the demon seat of the Ethereal Council. Who knew all it would take was this lone wolf to shove me off the fence? Granted, six months ago, I didn't know that it was one of seven Councils on this plane.

If I didn't know Barrett better, I'd say he arranged all this, but I did know better.

Marcus, however, looked like a proud papa. He put Finn in my path, knowing full well what I'd do when I figured out what a sack of shit he was. He knew I couldn't sit idly by and watch as he did it to someone else.

This was a test—one I'd passed without even knowing how I'd done it.

Turning back to the wolf in question, I nearly reveled in the confused horror on his face. Nearly, because enjoying this would make me no better than him, and I knew without a shadow of a doubt that reveling in his soon-to-be misery would sour my soul. But Finn couldn't go on like he had been. He couldn't keep preying on those he considered weak. He couldn't abuse his abilities like that without consequences. Not anymore.

"Finn, are you familiar with physics? Specifically, Newton's Third Law?"

His confusion only grew at my seemingly left turn to nowhere. Or maybe it was the physics talk.

"That's okay. I'll just tell you because I have a feeling you'll remember it for the rest of your life. Newton's Third Law is one of the cornerstones of modern physics. It states that every action has an equal and opposite reaction. Now, you've had too many actions with no appropriate reaction. Too many times where you have abused the power bestowed on you by the Fates. And today," I tsked, clucking my tongue at him, "you finally fucked with the wrong woman."

Finn's body coiled as if he were preparing to launch himself at me, but I was prepared for that. Before he could strike, I jabbed my three center fingers into his shirt at the line of his sternum just under a bronze pendant with a familiar symbol I couldn't place. I ripped that pendant off his neck, breaking the clasp at the same time, and threw it aside. Pressing the tips of my blunted fingernails in his chest, I forced myself not to rip the fabric or his skin, managing it by only the faintest of margins. My thumb and pinky fingers were spread wide, while the three center fingers pressed close together. Hand placement was key if I wanted to do this right.

At the touch of my fingers, Finn froze. He didn't blink. He didn't breathe. I didn't know if it was the power that flowed through my hands or his fear that solidified him to the spot.

"You attacked a Council member in full view of your pack and in witness of two other Council members. You attacked demon royalty and an unarmed woman without cause. You abused your power, against the orders of your Alpha and your pack. Punishment for these crimes is death, but I'm going to do you a favor. I'm not going to kill you. I'm going to give you the chance to change."

At those words, I pivoted my hand to the right like I was turning a key in a lock, feeling my power rise in me —not witch power, but something else. Something that I couldn't name, or maybe, I didn't want to name. This was the demon side I tried so hard not to tap into, the side that fed my witch half, made it so I didn't need an affinity to the moon or water or earth or fire or air. I didn't draw on anything but myself.

The ground beneath my feet began to quiver, and I hoped it wouldn't be like the courtroom incident. I didn't want to break the whole room apart just to teach this one man a lesson, but the walls stayed true, and the floor refused to crack. And even though I could feel the fear of every single wolf sing through me, I carried on.

I watched as the ice-blue aura above Finn's head sputtered and died. When the last flicker of light blinked out, Finn fell at my feet in a heap, sucking in a breath for the first time with his new lungs.

"Finnegan Lorenson, you are bound to this form, unable to reach your wolf. You will have a human lifespan, healing, senses, and strength. When you learn your lesson, when you understand that this life is a gift to be cherished, when you no longer wish to hurt those who you deem as weaker, come find me. Until then, make sure you work to learn from your mistakes. If you don't, you'll meet some of my family members in Hell, and I guarantee you they won't be as lenient."

Finn gurgled, a mix of rage and fear stealing his speech, and because he tried to kick me while I was down, I refused to do the same to him. Instead of stepping over him—which I really wanted to do because the bastard really had tried to kick me when I was splayed on the mat like a two-day-old fish—I skirted around his heap of man meat. That didn't stop me from skipping like a kid back to Barrett and Marcus, despite the voices buzzing like bees behind me.

I just did something impossible. Again. In front of a boatload of people who might like me a little but didn't have a single reason to be loyal to me at all. Making enemies wherever I went—that sure was a specialty of mine.

Marcus' warm hand circled my bicep, stopping me from bolting from the room which was my only plan past neutralizing the Viking asshole. His hold was gentle but insistent, and I couldn't bring myself to look at him. Instead, I met Barrett's gaze, the pride there soured a little by the fear.

"Settle down." Marcus' words were clear, his voice only barely raised, but the Alpha in him, the command in his voice, silenced the room in an instant. "If you think Maxima did this without my consent, you are sorely mistaken. Finn has been begging for punishment since he came to this pack, and his actions today against her should have earned her the right to take his head.

She gave us all a gift by punishing him without the loss of life."

That's when I realized Finn had been more than reckless. If he hadn't charged me, if he'd waited to attack and I hadn't judged him then, I wondered if Marcus would have had to kill him later. Suppressing a shudder, I homed in on the almost grateful tone to his voice weaving through the Alpha command.

"I want you to remember how few wolves there are in this world. I want you to remember our numbers. We are many here, but so many packs are few. This is a gift, a way not to lose another brother. Remember that."

I did a good thing. *I did*. But why did I feel like even though my actions were just, I was still going to pay for them anyway?

CHAPTER THREE

The same shifters who smiled at me yesterday looked anywhere but in my direction as I stalked down the hallway. Hell, they practically parted like the Red Sea. Just what I needed. A whole pack of shifters either scared of me, or worse—pissed off. It didn't matter if Barrett wanted me to start getting ready, I was leaving this house before Marcus' entire pack decided I was a better option for lunch.

Sweat-stained and bedraggled, I decided I couldn't look much worse than I already did. Why not add a hike through a valley in the middle of Colorado during the ass end of June on top of it? I raised my hand, ready to snap my fingers for all they were worth. How many times had I transported myself this way? A hundred? A thousand? More? It was as easy as blinking and just about as fast, letting the magic that coursed through my veins do the dirty work.

"Not so fast," Barrett called before I followed through. "Where do you think you're going?"

Did I want to explain? *No, I did not.*

"I wanted to see Bernadette," I offered lamely.

What I really wanted to say was that I missed my grandmother and wanted her to tell me everything was going to be okay. I hadn't spoken to her in ages, not since me and a couple of friends slaughtered a horde of Corax demons and stopped one of her sons from murdering her. My father was MIA—standard, really, after a lifetime or ten of him bailing unless he needed something —and she was the only person I really had to teach me what I needed to know.

About being on the Council. About being a demon. About what it was to be this freak of nature anomaly that shouldn't even exist.

You know, *the basics.*

"She isn't there."

My heart fell, but what did I expect? She hadn't been there the last ten times I tried to visit—why would she be there now? The cabin always appeared tiny on the outside, but under heavy cloaking and some probable time-slash-space continuum wizardry, it was anything but small on the inside. Nestled in the middle of a gorgeous valley barren of roads, very few people knew it was there. Or at least they didn't before an angel that shall not be named opened her big, fat trap.

Letting out a sigh that could rival a teenager's, I relaxed my fingers. I wasn't snapping my way out of this one.

"She isn't coming tonight, is she?" I already knew the answer.

She loved Samael. And I'd killed him. I'd gone into that battle knowing there would be repercussions. I just never expected her refusing to talk to me to be one of them.

"I don't think so," Barrett whispered, crossing the length of the corridor to me.

I'd like to think he was offering comfort, and maybe a part of him was, but I had an inkling that he was trying to keep me from bolting and blowing my entire Ethereal future to smithereens.

"She blames me for Samael. For destroying her escape. Doesn't she?"

Of course she did. Not only did I kill my uncle, but I also crushed the bone blade to dust. I'd taken away her only chance to die in peace. Hell, I'd hate me, too.

"She'll get over it."

I rolled my eyes. "I killed her son, Barrett. That isn't a thing you just get over."

Barrett's expression went from consoling to grave. "If you hadn't done it, if you hadn't killed him, one of us would have. He earned that death." Barrett's hands landed on top of my shoulders, holding me in place so I actually met his eyes. "You saved the lives of hundreds of thousands, maybe millions of people. You stopped a war that has been brewing since the dawn of time. She'll get over it."

I shrugged, and Barrett got me moving, steering me to the room I'd be tortured in for the next twelve hours.

"No more stalling. It's time to get this show on the road."

"I'M SORRY, MAX."

Marcus' gravelly voice broke through the swirling deliberation bouncing around my skull, and I stopped staring into the mirror for a second to really look at him. This was the third time he'd apologized, and unless I got my shit together, he was just going to keep doing it.

It wasn't his fault. None of it, but he would shoulder the blame all the same because that was what an Alpha did. Also, his husband was a fucking menace.

I was sitting on a spindly-looking stool in what had to be a great aunt's wet dream of a dressing room.

Staring into the Hollywood-style mirror, I assessed the damage. I was all for getting dolled up, and I could do a painted lip and winged eye with the best of them, but this was something else. This was a level of primping I had yet to achieve, and still, I looked about the same.

Or at least, I saw myself under the layers of gold eyeshadow, false lashes, and gold-inlaid body oils that made my already-bronze skin practically glow. I'd been buffed and shined like a new penny, my hair had been curled and tamed, and through all of it, I hadn't gotten one lick of a say.

But this was going too damn far.

"You want me to do what now?" My voice cracked a bit, but I didn't blame myself in the least.

"It's tradition. Everything I've done so far has been tradition," Barrett insisted, exasperated, even though he wasn't the one being pulled and stretched like a damn Thanksgiving turkey.

I called bullshit. "No. In no way is this dress, these shoes, this makeup, tradition. This ceremony is for babies, Barrett. Unless you're putting false eyelashes on an infant, none of this has been tradition. There is no fucking way I am—"

"They insisted."

They. The Fates had screwed with me yet again, only this time, it was in a super-gross way. Everything would be hunky dory if I weren't about to get painted with blood.

"Of course they insisted. It's gross, I don't want to do it, and it's going to piss me off. It's their *modus operandi*. Do they have it out for me, or is this just for kicks?"

Barrett sighed for approximately the three thousandth time. "This is tradition. Every babe that goes through those doors has to be claimed by blood."

He was talking about the doors to the grand ballroom, the same ones I would walk through by myself because Bernadette wouldn't be there with me. Neither would my parents or my sister or my friends. Sure, Maria, Striker, and Della would be there at the end, but I was walking in alone.

Focusing on the bowl of familial blood in Barrett's hands, a thought struck me. "Whose blood is that?"

An expression crossed Barrett's face like he would rather be boiled alive in a vat of oil than answer me. "Andras donated to the cause."

Andras. My father. The bastard who'd gotten me burned at the stake. The giant flaming asshole who tanked my life on purpose. I parted my lips to protest.

"Don't. Just don't. Do you think you're not going to walk in there with every single person judging you? Do you honestly think I'm going to let you walk into that ballroom without every single facet of your appearance on point? You are a former Rogue, Maxima. Add on top of that your lineage, and every single molecule of your being will be weighed and measured and assessed. By every person who is there tonight. Including the Fates. Hell, especially the Fates."

"And if I don't let you primp me within an inch of my life, I'm going to offend some ancient Ethereal being who will probably want to skin me alive on principle. Right?"

Barrett sighed for the three thousandth and one time. "Essentially."

Just pretend it's chicken blood. *Gag.* No, pretend it's paint. *Yeah, that's better.*

"Fine." I conceded, but I could tell I looked green.

"Oh, give it a rest. It's only a few drops mixed with face and body paint. No need to get all squeamish."

He probably could have told me that at the beginning instead of dragging out all this drama, but whatever.

Something else occurred to me, but I had to wait until Barrett dragged the broad, ornamental brush down the center of my face before I could ask, the coppery tang filling my nostrils. *A few drops, my ass.* He whispered as he painted a thick, straight line down the center of my face, words so faint I couldn't make them out, but hoped it was a blessing.

"Because I'm dual-natured, will both sides of myself

be represented or only the one? I know I'm a freak of nature anomaly and everything, but walking in there denying my witch heritage seems…" I trailed off, unable to articulate precisely why not representing my witch side would be a bad thing.

"Wrong?" Marcus supplied the simplest of answers to the question still rooting around in my skull.

I nodded. "Wrong."

Barrett pressed his lips together, indecision on his face as he set the bowl and brush down. "You know that means asking Teresa, don't you?"

My mother and I would never be best buddies or have the sort of loving relationship rom-coms were made of, but sometime after she blessed my friends and I, we managed to find some kind of a truce. This was something she should have done four hundred years ago when I was born. Now she could finally make good.

That was, if she'd do it.

"Which one of us has to do the asking?" I threw the question out there, letting it settle. And if I also happened to shamelessly put my brown puppy-dog eyes to work, I had no regrets.

Barrett assessed my pleading expression, harrumphed, turned, and then gave blue puppy eyes to his husband.

"Oh, come on!" Marcus groused, before catching the

full force of both Barrett's and my pitiful stares. I even threw in a whimper for good measure.

"Fine! I'll ask her, but if she says no, you two are just going to have to deal."

"Thanks, Marcus!" I called to his back as he slipped from the room to call my mother.

Not five minutes later, Marcus stalked back into the room with my mother striding right behind him, the short train of her burgundy dress trailing behind her.

I couldn't recall my mother ever wearing a dress like this one. It had a high, jeweled neckline and long sleeves, but the major thing that kept it from being frumpy was the way the fabric hugged her curves all the way to the top of her hips before falling in a straight column.

Then she walked past me to an altar set up inside one of those roll-top desks, and I got a load of the rest of it. Backless. Completely backless. Mom looked hot.

Once I got over her dress, I paid attention to what she was doing.

Pulling a knife from who knew where, she cut her palm just like they did in the movies, letting the blood flow into a small stone bowl. First off, why? And second? That spot was just about the worst place to cut, ever. It took forever to heal, and the scars jacked with all the palmistry lines.

I wanted to ask, but as soon as she got the nod from Barrett that she provided enough, she snapped her fingers, and the blood slowed before stopping altogether, the cut healing in a matter of seconds.

She really needed to teach me that one.

Once her cut was a thing of the past, she spirited the knife away into a sheath at her thigh, and turned to walk back out the room without ever saying a word to me or acknowledging me at all.

"Mom," I called before she could leave, and at that single word, she halted in a stutter-step as if my lone word was a command.

Teresa turned back to me, her eyes shiny with unshed tears. "I'll see you out there, okay?"

I wanted to ask her if I was doing the right thing. I wanted to know if she was proud of me. I wanted to know if she cared at all.

But I didn't ask.

And she didn't say.

CHAPTER FOUR

My heels clicked on the pale-blue marble floors of the grand ballroom, a room I'd never seen in Aether—which didn't mean much. Too many of the rooms in the underground witch club didn't actually belong to the building itself but were doorways to somewhere else. The vast ballroom seemed to go on forever, the ceilings domed and painted and at least three-stories high. Wide marble columns sat at thirty-foot intervals along the sides of the room, and in between each stood groups of well-dressed partygoers.

Was that the right term? Partygoer? This was a ball of sorts, but more than that, it was my presentation to the Fates. Should I call them spectators, revelers, witnesses? In all likelihood, they were here for the free food, free drinks, and the spectacle of a four-hundred-year-old demon-hybrid finally showing up to what was sort of like an Ethereal christening.

This was for babies. Not grown women. It showed in the fact that I hadn't had a say in what I wore, or what makeup I had on, or the painted line of demon blood that bisected one side of my face from the other. That and the trail of witch blood that ran from one temple, over the top of my cheekbones, across my nose, curving up to the other temple. I didn't choose the crown on my head, or the shoes on my feet, or the jewelry at my ears. None of it.

That wasn't to say that the dress, jewelry, shoes, and the crown weren't beautiful and of the highest quality. They were. Barrett had excellent taste.

But they weren't mine. This place wasn't mine— these people weren't mine.

The only thing that *was* mine was the ink tattooed into my skin. That, they couldn't take away, but somehow it made me even more of a spectacle than I already was. This dress—Grecian in style —had a wide V-neck and back, reaching almost to my navel, my skin exposed to the room. My tattooed sleeves, the mandala under my breasts, the flowers and vines on my back, hell, even the giant dragon that started at my ribs and wound down and around my hip to the top of my left thigh, peeked out of the indigo fabric. The slits of the floor-length skirt parted with every step, showing more skin than I liked. And while the dress itself was beautiful, a part of me wondered about the golden scales at my shoulders that held the fabric together—wondered if they were real dragon scales or if they were replicas. I prayed they weren't real, but I didn't have much hope. Given the blood painted on my face, I wouldn't put it past them at this point.

I felt naked and exposed and on display—when given the fact that this was a presentation, made sense, but I didn't like it.

My heels—sky-high, golden, strappy, flimsy little things—still clicked, echoing through the silent room. I'd never been in a room filled with so many people that was this quiet. It was eerie and proof positive that there couldn't be a single human in the bunch. They all aped human well enough, and even though I kept my face forward, I saw the glamours and magics out of the corner of my eye.

Power buffeted me on both sides, the shiver of it all buzzing against my skin, but never more than the energy I was walking toward.

At the center of the room, a compass was laid into the marble, the giant spines pointing north to the three women I was here to meet. The trio was perched on a raised dais with three golden thrones, each at an equal height which felt significant for some reason, as if they ruled in concert and not separately. But I knew this already, didn't I? Barrett made sure I read up on all the lore regarding those three. Not because I would get tested, but so I wouldn't stick my foot in my mouth and shit all over his meticulous planning.

As I got closer, I realized the three women looked nothing like what I thought they would. For starters, they didn't appear to be women at all. At best I would classify them as adolescents, but even I knew that looks could be deceiving. I supposed looking like a teenager would be preferable to looking like an old crone. Many a person would underestimate a teen, not so much a seasoned lady with the roadmap of time written across her face.

Sneaky.

The one on the left was white-blonde, the middle one dark-haired, and the right one a redhead. None of them appeared older than eighteen, and even that was a push. They sat with a teenager's irreverence, lounging on their golden thrones without a care for the fancy clothes they wore or the importance of the situation. The Fates. The Moirai. Clotho, Lachesis, and Atropos didn't give a blue fuck about any of this. Well, neither did I, but I had to make a show of it, didn't I?

As I neared the end of my trek, my family and friends

came into view. Dressed to the nines, my motley crew of supporters was a sight for sore eyes. Unlike the others in the room that stuck to their own kind, my group was a mix of nearly all species of Ethereal. My sister, Maria, a full-blooded witch, stood front and center, buffeted on both sides by Striker, an angel and something mixed that was probably dragon, if I had a guess, and Aidan, a full-blooded wraith. Next to them was Aurelia Constantine, my phoenix BFF, Della, my vampire assistant-slash-bodyguard, and my mother, Teresa. I was amazed Aurelia was standing that close to my mom, but since neither of them were bloody, I wasn't going to question it.

I had so many who were here to support me, I tried to stomp down the hurt that Bernadette was nowhere to be seen. My father was here, why couldn't she be?

Ten feet from the dais, I stopped to let my parents step forward, the choreographed steps Barrett had hammered into my brain for the last six months, my mother to the left, my father to the right, and we walked in step the last little bit, waiting for the three women to acknowledge us. Then we waited a bit more.

I racked my brain to try and remember the steps Barrett had gone over and over and *over* to make sure I didn't mess up, but no. I wasn't supposed to do anything else. These women—Deities? Gods? Assholes?—were the ones who were supposed to get this show on the road. I had a nearly irresistible urge to tap my foot, but I figured that wouldn't be too good for my health such as it was. The whole reason I was here was so I *didn't* piss these women off, and it was a reason I had to repeat in my head so I wouldn't let my mouth get me into trouble.

"All this fuss and she disrespects us so," the redhead hissed, her voice not carrying much past where my parents and I stood. Shifting in her seat to lean over to the dark-haired one's ear, she whispered there for a second before the dark-haired one finally glanced up from her inspection of her nails.

"Is this the thanks we get for putting up with this drivel? Tainted blood on display for the world to see?" the dark one asked as if I knew what the hell they were talking about.

"Can't you two see she has no idea what you're talking about?" the white-haired one joined in, removing her legs from her armrest and sitting up to examine me. "The poor little child has no clue what it means to be what she is. The least we can do is ask her why she decided displaying the cursed Arcadios blood was a way to honor us."

Great. Arcadios blood. My mother's blood. Why in the holy hell would they be offended at the sight of my mother's blood?

"Fine, Clotho, but the offense has been noted," the redhead replied.

"So be it, Atropos, note away."

So, the white-haired one was Clotho, the spinner, the favorite. The dark-haired one was Lachesis, the measurer, the forgotten, and the redhead was Atropos, the cutter, the inflexible.

And somehow—without even speaking, mind you—I'd already pissed them off. Aces.

"We reside here today to accept the presentation of a child. Who amongst you is here to give over your child to the will of the Moirai? Who here is prepared to give your child over to the Fates of man and Ethereal alike?" the three Fates asked in unison.

My parents linked their arms with mine and took the last step forward.

"We present you this child, Moirai, born many years ago, so you may see to her thread, so you may weave it as you will." Andras said the words Barrett said he would.

"We present you this child, sisters of Fate, so you may guide her on her journey, and measure out the longest of threads," Teresa said her part.

The three had no problem when my father spoke, but when Teresa said her part, two of the three sneered the way only a teenager could, full of ripe condescension and distaste.

Now it was my turn, and I didn't know if their contempt of my mother would transfer to me. I had a feeling it would. "Clotho, Lachesis, Atropos, I present myself to you, in witness of these fine families, so you may determine my worth and measure accordingly. I present the blood of my father, Crown Prince Andras, and the blood of my mother, High Priestess of the Pacific Northwest Covens, Teresa Alcado. I present the blood that makes my family, both lines of it, so you may judge *both* sides of me. The demon side and the witch side."

That last bit wasn't in the script, but with their distaste, I had to make a stand for the blood painted on my skin—had to let them know that even with their objections, that blood was still mine.

Lachesis seemed appeased at my explanation, but Atropos narrowed her eyes, irritation blooming across her fair skin like a rose—and this rose had some mighty big thorns. It seemed like a bad sign that the "cutter of the thread" was pissed off at me.

Before Atropos could decide my thread needed an immediate shearing, Clotho spoke. "You honor us, child. By displaying both of your lines, you show us where your heart lies.

Lachesis picked up where her sister left off. "You honor us as you stand united as a family."

Atropos paused before she opened her mouth, a calculating little smile on her face. She seemed eager to draw out this game as long as possible. Maybe to see if I'd break and tell her to fuck off, maybe to see if I could actually act like an adult. Who knew the mind of an ancient woman stuck choosing when everyone would die?

Irritated that I picked today of all days to act like a full-fledged adult complete with self-control, she said in the most monotonous voice ever. "You honor us with your presentation."

Then her face twisted into an evil grin. "As a favor to the Moirai, we request that you dance with any male that asks you on this fine night. You may not turn a single one away."

Request. This wasn't a request. This was an order thinly veiled as a favor. Denying her, pissing her off even more, didn't seem like an option I was willing to entertain. I was going to have to just suck it up. I'd been doing it all damn day—why not just keep the charade going?

But by the reception in this room, I had a feeling Atropos just set me up for one crapshoot of a night.

Yippee.

CHAPTER FIVE

My father was the first man to ask me to dance, which given the severe faces in the room, was almost a blessing. Andras and I weren't on too good of terms. You know, after I killed his brother and made sure the bone blade everyone and their momma was fighting over was destroyed. To my credit, his brother was an evil douche canoe who wanted to start the Apocalypse, so I didn't feel too bad. Honestly, I'd killed for far less.

But Andras didn't seem bothered about the last time we spoke. He had an almost dewy-eyed glow to his face that made me pause for a slight moment once the music started. He clasped my hand in his, wrapped a sure arm around my back, and led me out into a waltz so perfect, it was proof he'd been around long before the dance was invented.

He led me through the paces of the slow ballad remake of an '80s song. "You look confused."

"Not confused, I just don't know what that expression is," I answered honestly.

Andras smiled, his eyes glowing yellow for a moment. "It's pride, sweetheart. I'm sorry this is the first time you're seeing it. I'm proud of you, of what you did. I was pissed at the time, but you did what I couldn't. And this is all I wanted for you. To take your place here, to be recognized once the danger had passed. It took far longer than I wanted it to, but I'm glad I'm here to see it."

Parental pride was a new thing for me, and I wasn't sure what I was supposed to say back. Unable to find the right words, I nodded as he led me through the first turn, then settled on snark. "No offense, but who are you, and what have you done with my dickhead of a dad?"

Andras chuckled, a rueful smile tempering my insult. "I suppose I deserve that. To be honest, being a good guy isn't my normal setting. But this is the first time I'm not in the middle of preventing a war, so maybe this is who I'm supposed to be. Who knows?"

He paused, leading me through another turn. "I just

wanted to make sure you knew all the good stuff, because some of the men you dance with tonight are going to be complete dicks to you. They're going to look down on you because of your bloodline, because you're a woman, because of who you are. They are going to say shit to you because you killed Samael, and Atropos knows it. She hates your mother and her bloodline, and if she can fuck with you, she will."

"Goodie. I so wanted to be on the bad side of the woman who controls my death," I said dryly.

Andras stifled a laugh but couldn't prevent his lips from turning up at my sarcasm. "I wanted the first thing you heard out here to be good, because you're about to get a whole truckload of unpleasant. Do your best not to lose it. That's the end goal, you know. To make sure you display that you're unfit for the Council seat."

My father held me closer, an almost hug in the middle of the formal dance and whispered in my ear, "Don't let her win."

Andras was warning me, and if Atropos' sneer was anything to go by, he was right to. All too soon, the song ended, and a youngish brown-haired man bowed to my father before holding his hand out to me. I took it without hesitation, refusing to let my reluctance show. I wouldn't give Atropos the satisfaction.

"Maxima Arcadios. At last, we finally meet."

His voice was smooth as silk and just as rich, knocking up his attractiveness at least five degrees. His shoulder-length hair bogged him down, but his eyes were kind enough.

"It's just Max. And I don't use the Arcadios name."

He seemed bemused at my correction. "All the same, it's Arcadios blood in your veins and on your face. You're an Arcadios witch whether you call yourself one or not. Bold move, by the way."

"What?"

"Nodding to your witch half. The Arcadios line isn't as accepted as some, but the honor is there. We witches won't forget it."

"So you're a witch, then?" I asked only because I had to. My dance partner was cloaking himself in the most epic way possible, and I couldn't even see the magic he was using to do it, a fact that was less and less comforting the more I thought about it. But he only nodded and didn't offer any more information.

"Are you in a coven? I always wondered how those really worked. Is it like a family?"

Bemused, my dance partner smiled again. "In all the best and worst ways. You have backup, but no privacy and everything is run by committee. But no, I'm not in a coven."

"Oh, sorry. Was my question rude? I'm afraid I'm a bit ignorant on Ethereal social norms."

"Don't worry about it. I'm sure you'll learn soon enough."

My mind went fuzzy for a second, and the next thing I knew, I was dancing with a new partner. My steps stuttered, and I accidentally stepped on his toe.

"Sorry," I whispered, trying not to catch the attention of the other dancers swarming around us.

When had the dance floor filled up? And who decided sea salt cologne was a good idea? A ton of humans thought it was a pleasant smell, but the scent always made my hackles rise. The stronger it hung in the air, the more likely someone was fucking with someone else's mind. I shuddered again, and I tread on my partner's other foot.

"Fates, woman. Can't you do a simple box step?" my partner growled through his teeth.

My new dance partner was tall and broad. Fiery dark-red hair was brushed back off his face, highlighting the spray of freckles peppering his skin, and his eyes were an unearthly shade of orange that I'd only seen on one other kind of Ethereal.

Demons.

Still puzzled on how I'd gone from dancing with my father to this gem, I concentrated on my steps and tried to ignore him. Sure, he was attractive, most Ethereals were, but adding in his attitude with the general contempt on his face, I figured we probably wouldn't be friends.

"You try dancing on these toothpicks called shoes. *Excuse* me."

He sneered, his orange eyes glowing amber, either with his power or from the eerie lighting in the ballroom.

"Complete waste of my time. There is no way someone like *you* is taking the Council seat. This whole thing is a complete farce."

Someone like me? You mean the woman who already took the damn job? I wanted to inform him of that fact but decided against it. If Barrett hadn't told anyone that I had the job, I didn't want to spoil it.

"Golly gee. Tell me how you really feel." I rolled my eyes. "What was your name again?"

"Donovan." He seethed, his jaw clenched tight enough I saw the flex in the muscle.

"Let's see, you don't like me for the Council seat because I have a vagina, right? Or it's because I've been a Rogue for the last four hundred years? Oh, I know, it's because I'm a half-breed, and my tainted-bloodness is stealing the seat out from under you?"

His eyes widened at "vagina" but went positively

glacial when I mentioned stealing the seat. *Ding-ding-ding. We have a winner.*

"That's it. But see, they like someone like me for the seat because I'm not a flaming asshole with a superiority complex. Maybe you should work on your people skills, and you'll get it next time." I smiled, just waiting for my dance partner—*err*—*Donovan* to lose his mind in front of all these people.

Before Donny could lose it, a handsome Asian man swiftly cut in, stealing me away and leaving Donovan standing on the dance floor in the middle of the twirling masses.

"Aww, no fair. I wanted to see him explode," I whined, and my new dance partner chuckled.

"That is the exact reason I stole you away. It's for your own safety, Princess," the man said, but it seemed more like a joke to him than anything else, so I let the princess name-calling slide.

"You don't sound American. Where are you from, mystery savior?"

A smile bloomed once again on his strikingly handsome face, his eyes crinkling and everything. "England by way of Malaysia. And as much as I like the title 'mystery savior,' I prefer the name Felix if you don't mind."

"Felix, like the cat?" I tried to get a rise out of him. I'd never seen someone so carefree.

"Felix like the cat," he returned without even a hint of derision. "I work with Donovan and have for some time. He isn't suited for the Council, and he knows it, but he's one of three others —myself included—who are in line for the seat. Now, I don't see myself as a Councilman, so you won't be hearing a cross word from me."

Interesting. I didn't know there was anyone else in line for the seat other than myself, but leave it to Barrett to neglect to tell me these things. But Felix didn't need to know I'd already taken the seat, and he also didn't need to know I had no idea if I even should have. He seemed to know way more than I did about Ethereal goings-on.

"So you work with Donovan. What do you do?" I asked instead.

Felix grinned, full of pride, the smile colored with just a hint of evil. "We're Knights of Hell. All three of the potentials are. Donovan, myself, and Alistair. We guard the gates keeping damned souls in where they belong."

I fought not to raise my eyebrows in complete disbelief. I found it hard to believe this smiling, happy man was a guardian of the gates of Hell. He didn't look mean enough to guard the doors of a Chuck E. Cheese.

"And I suppose that impresses all the ladies."

Felix shrugged noncommittally as he led me through another turn. "It doesn't hurt."

"So Donovan is the surly one, you're the pleasant one—what does that make Alistair? Is he going to bite my head off and feed me to a Corax?"

Felix winced, his pained expression making me wonder if it was the Corax talk or Alistair himself that was causing his discomfort.

"Alistair is the perpetually irritated one. Donovan is just a hothead who didn't want to come to this thing in the first place. Alistair actually wants the job. He's pretty pissed off you came onto the scene since your claim is higher than his."

Felix was a veritable fount of gossip. I needed to keep this little gem in my hip pocket. Barrett might not know all this demon-y hierarchy nonsense.

"I did stop the Apocalypse. Doesn't that earn me some brownie points?"

"Depends on who you talk to. Demons love a good war." Felix sighed wistfully as if war was something to pine after.

Soon, the song ended, and another man asked me to dance. I endured three minutes of judgment from a man who was probably older than dirt. My feet ached, the shoes ill-suited for constant wear and little to no sitting time. Luckily, after that song ended, I stole away before anyone else could ask me to take another spin. Plucking a champagne flute from a passing waiter's tray, I slowly sipped it even though I really wanted to chug. Positively parched, I glanced around for a non-alcoholic option once my glass was empty. The last thing I needed was more champagne on an empty stomach.

"Looking for the hors d'oeuvres?" a man asked from behind me, and I couldn't help the sigh of defeat that passed my lips at the sound of his cultured British accent.

I was going to get asked to dance. Again. And probably mocked. Super.

"Yes," I said almost pitifully, turning to get a better look at the man I would probably be dancing with in a few minutes.

After I got some food, of course.

Since I was in heels, he wasn't too much taller than me, maybe six feet or so with a pair of baby blues that could make a girl weep. Artfully tousled reddish-brown hair accentuated his high cheekbones, and then adding in his damn near pouty lips, well, let's just say he wasn't hard to look at. Plus, the man filled out a suit.

He was hot, but it seemed all Ethereals were hot. Looking back at all my encounters over the centuries, every single Ethereal had been attractive, and since most of us didn't age, we would all just go on being hot forever. The orgies in Aether were starting to make more sense.

It took me a second to realize the man had just been staring at me, and me at him. In silence. Awkward.

Shaking myself, I started talking, and just couldn't stop. "I haven't had a thing to eat since sparring with a bunch of werewolves this morning. This is my first ball or dance or gala or whatever, and no one tells you how long it takes to get ready or how long these things last. I mean, really, I could eat a steak as big as my face right now."

My potential dance partner seemed like he was holding in a smile.

"Sorry. That is probably the single glass of champagne working its way through my system. If you would like to dance, I promise to try not to talk your ear off."

He let his smile go, and I swear to the Fates, I almost swooned. Dimples. The man had dimples. He held out his elbow for me to take and led me back to the dance floor where one of my favorite songs by Bonhom was playing. Mystery dance partner led me into a waltz, which was standard fare for the night, the long steps a perfect placement for the haunting song.

"I'm Max, by the way," I offered when he didn't say anything for what seemed like a full minute.

"I know." A smile stretched his mouth again, as if he

knew a secret I didn't. Of course he did. He actually knew his name.

"You see, I told you my name in the hopes you would tell me yours. Unlike everyone else in this room, I haven't been around the upper crust for the last bazillion years, so I don't know anyone. Including you."

"You could just ask, you know," he said offhandedly as he led me into a turn and then back into his space again.

"Fine." I sighed, trying for stern. "What's your name?"

He chuckled. "I don't know if I want to tell you. You probably know it already and all the gossip that follows it."

"I promise I don't. If we haven't met before, I probably know nothing about you. Honest."

"All right. If you insist on knowing your dance partner, I'm Alistair Quinn."

I was wrong. I did know that name.

This was the man who wanted my job.

CHAPTER SIX

"So, you do know me." Alistair assessed my expression, a smug half-smile pulling at his lips. "Good. Then you know why I'm here."

Why he was here was the unknown part. Did he just want to square up to the person who had the job he wanted? But he didn't know I'd already taken the job, did he? He thought he was still in the running.

Did I want to tell him?

I took in his dimpled half-smile and arrogant expression. *No, I didn't want to tell him.* I wanted him to put his foot in it and then brandish the mother of all trump cards, watching his face as it crumpled in defeat. Yes, that would be much more satisfying.

"I know your name and profession. And I learned

both of those tonight from your friend, Felix. I understand you're irritated I was asked to take the position?"

Alistair's expression hardened like I expected it to. "You mean, am I irritated that some upstart with exactly zero knowledge of our ways and customs was asked to take the most venerated seats available for our kind? No." He mocked sarcastically. "Why would I give a ripe shite about demon politics?"

"I might not know all the ways and customs, but can't you even for a second consider that maybe that's a good thing? I don't know the history, so I will always choose what is right and wrong. Not based on history but based on now. I won't have eons of prejudice clouding every decision."

"How could you possibly know what is right and wrong if you have no understanding of the reasons behind the actions you'll be judging?"

I scoffed. "Because I won't be the only person doing the judging? It's a Council, it's not like I'll be alone destroying lives willy-nilly." A man like him wouldn't even consider that someone like me could have anything to offer. "You probably think I'm being served this job on a damn platter. I've been on this planet for four centuries amongst humans, watching every war, every atrocity. If you think I'm some vapid little child, you're sorely mistaken."

"Yes, amongst humans. You don't know the first thing about demons." He sneered, ignoring my argument altogether while he expertly led me through and around the other dancers. His form was perfect, which irritated me almost as much as his snobby attitude.

But he had to know just how evil humans could be. He was a Knight of Hell. His job was to keep the vilest of souls right where they belonged.

"Maybe so, but weren't demons created to punish the wicked? Isn't that our purpose? Humans can't be all sunshine and roses if the powers that be deigned to create a whole realm just to weed out the bad seeds. You even have the job of keeping the craftiest from escaping. Even if I think you're probably horrible at your job, you have to agree humans are nothing to sneeze at."

Alistair's pale face reddened in affront. *Yeah, I said it.* If he were any good at his job, I wouldn't have died in front of all my friends two years ago. I wouldn't have lost so much. I wouldn't still dream about the life leaking out of me that night.

"What in Fate's name makes you think I'm not the best at my job?" He seethed through clenched teeth.

"Do the names Baron, Bella, and Tessa Bishop mean anything to you?" I saw his sneer and raised him one. *Knight of Hell. Pfft.*

Alistair's steps stuttered before his surprise morphed

into something akin to rage. Leading me off the dance floor, he grabbed my upper arm in a blisteringly hot hand, the ironclad grip brooking no argument. I was following him. Or else. Damn demons and their penchant for burning. Alistair steered me toward a darkened corner of the ballroom, assumingly where he could chastise me without prying ears.

Well, fuck that.

Ignoring the pain, I picked right up where I left off on the dance floor. "Those names should sound real familiar. Baron and Bella tried to spring their mother from Hell by attacking the three pieces of the Veil. You know, the three beings that keep Heaven, Hell, and the Otherside from crashing into this plane. You remember those, right? I died trying to stop them. In fact, I still remember exactly how it felt, still dream about it. If you were any good at your job, you would be protecting both sides of the gates, and not leaving us to do your work for you. *That's* how I know you're shit at your job."

I snatched my arm out of his hold. "And watch your temperature, *Knight*. Burn me again, and it won't be Andras you'll need to fear." I stepped into his space, making sure my threat was clear as crystal. "It'll be me."

Stepping back, I tried not to let the fear fill me as I scanned my arms for brands. Micah managed to brand me with a single burning hand. I'd hate to have to kill Alistair, but I would before I let anyone own me.

"I didn't"—He paused before clearing his throat and lowering his voice—"I didn't mean to burn you. Please let me see."

His touch was gentle as he inspected my bicep. Red, raised skin in the shape of his large hand encircled my arm, and he let out a hiss under his breath. "I'll fix it. I swear. I didn't mean to hurt you. I didn't know"—He paused again and let out a sigh—"I forgot you are not inured to the heat."

"You thought I wouldn't burn." I chuckled, even though the scorched skin hurt like a sonofabitch. "You don't know much about me, do you?"

Confusion clouded his expression. "Why would burning be comical?" he asked as he inspected the skin.

"Because I was burned at the stake? It's how I became a Rogue in the first place. All this piss and vinegar about me taking your rightful spot, and you don't know the first thing about me, do you?"

His jaw clenched as my point hit home. "I know enough. I also know how to fix this, but you'll have to stay still."

He raised a thumb to his mouth, and I caught the barest glimpse of fangs before they sliced into the flesh. He brought the bloody digit to the burn, and before I could protest, he'd drawn a full circle of blood through the middle of the wound. Instantly, the pain abated, and I watched with wide eyes as the red, raised skin melted away to my normal bronze coloring.

"This didn't bind me to you or magically marry us, or some other bullshit, right? Because I've had about enough of that to last a lifetime."

Alistair's eyebrows raised again as if I'd surprised him. He really *didn't* know anything about me.

"A demon bound you?" At my nod, pure malice washed across his face. "Who?"

"Don't worry, Knight, it didn't take." I brushed off his concern. The last thing I needed was another man worrying about me, even if it was this prick.

"So, you killed him, then?" Alistair accused, and instantly, I bristled.

I didn't deserve that tone, but I couldn't erupt on the man in front of all these people even if we were off the beaten path. I didn't feel an ounce of guilt for killing Micah, and I never would. I'd have killed him twice if I could have. Too bad Andras beat me to the punch.

"Wouldn't be the first man I taught not to take things that didn't belong to him. Study up, Knight, there's a whole host of stuff you don't know about me."

With that, I eyed the closest exit and made my way there. I didn't care where the doors actually took me, I just needed to get the hell out of here. Maybe to a place with food and a seat. But I didn't make it that far. Instead, a warm grip snagged my hand and pulled me back around.

Alistair. Again.

Only this time his grip was gentle, and his expression wasn't accusing. It was open—*and I daresay*—even honest. And still, he pulled me closer to him.

"I want to know who bound you." His voice was a gravelly husk of the posh British accent he'd had just minutes ago. His irises glowed amber, and the tips of his fangs flashed just behind his lips. "Tell me who did that to you."

"Why do you need to know? It's none of your concern, *Knight*." I used his title like a slur, but Alistair wasn't taking the bait.

"I give a shit, that's why. No one deserves to be bound without their consent. But especially, not someone like you."

"You mean a Princess? Like those of a lower station don't matter?"

Alistair sighed. "You could aggravate a saint, couldn't you?"

He had no idea. "It's a gift. Now let go of my hand and let me go get some food."

His grip tightened just slightly before his hand fell

away. But that didn't mean he let me go. Oh, no. He just stepped closer, getting in my space in a way I couldn't ignore him, holding me there without even touching me.

"I'm not letting you go anywhere until I know the demon who did that to you is dead. And if he's not, I plan to make him that way post haste."

I didn't know why he cared. As far as I knew, Alistair Quinn wanted the job I already had, and other than that, he didn't have one thing to do with me.

"Don't worry, I took care of it."

He rolled his eyes. "Just give me the name, Max."

He wanted his name? Sure, I'd give it to him. I supposed he didn't need to know it was never Micah's idea to come after me. It was Ruby's. And it probably wasn't her idea, either. The list kept growing into a web of people I couldn't trust, couldn't find, or couldn't forget. Micah and Samael were dead, but Ruby... I'd been looking for her for six months, and it was as if she'd dropped off the face of the map.

But she didn't bind me, even if she'd sent him after me. Micah did that all on his own.

"Fine. Micah Goode."

Alistair hissed in recognition. Good to know the man of my worst nightmares was famous. At least Ruby sent the cream of the crop after me.

"Don't worry about killing him, I took care of that

already, and when he came back as a spirit, Andras finished him off. But I'll tell you what, if he manages to come back another time, I'll let you have a crack at him."

"You've been taking care of yourself for a long time, haven't you?" His voice was little more than a whisper, but I heard him anyway.

He had no idea. I'd been taking care of myself long before I was ever a Rogue.

"You bet."

Something washed over his expression, and it took everything in me not to take that tiny step forward, not to get just that little bit farther into his space. But I couldn't go there with this man. Not now.

Maybe not ever.

"You're safe, right?"

Probably? Maybe? No, I most likely wasn't, but this man didn't need to know that, and it sure as hell wasn't his responsibility.

"Of course I am. Who'd want to kill me?" I smiled, but the fact of the matter was this whole thing was a joke. I didn't belong here in the middle of the ball or gala, or whatever the hell it was. I wasn't aristocracy, not really. I was a tattooed outcast who liked to make sure people paid for picking on the little guy.

And that's all I'd ever be. An avenging angel—or demon, as the case may be.

I managed to break away from Alistair, each step from him bringing clarity and a coldness I hadn't felt earlier. I needed more of it. I needed that chill in my blood and the sense that came with it. I needed a clear head and a free heart.

But most of all, I needed a quiet room. Chair optional.

The door led back to Aether proper, the pounding music rattling through my ribcage, and I struggled through throngs of bodies toward my destination. Strobe lights flashed, the heat filtering into my closely guarded chill. I headed toward the one door no one in their right mind would go to.

The Latin inscription above the door to the high courtroom called to me. *Numera omnes qui ingrediuntur ad iudicium. Judgment comes to all who enter.* I wanted to be here, a place I felt I belonged—a place where I could do a little bit of good, keeping an eye out for those little guys I cared so much about.

But the normally all-white, blindingly bright courtroom was dark.

"*Detrahet me in lucem.*" I snapped my fingers in the gloom. Light bloomed in my palm, and what I saw had me backing up to make sense of it.

A large swath of the formerly white courtroom was

splashed in red, the copper tang hitting me full in the face now that my brain supplied the word.

Blood.

A red-haired woman was splayed in the middle of the largest puddle, and it took me far too long to realize her hair wasn't red at all. It was blonde, stained scarlet from her blood.

I knew the woman, too. It was as if my mind conjured her from my most hideous of thoughts and plopped her exactly where I didn't want her. I'd longed for revenge on this woman, but in all my plans, I never wanted this.

But it seemed Ruby had one last "fuck you" for me, especially with the message, "A gift for the princess," spelled out in blood, painted on the steps of the dais of the high court.

I was going to get blamed for this. I just knew it.

CHAPTER SEVEN

I wasn't looking at the dead woman on the floor. Nope. My eyes were trained on the crudely drawn message staining the white marble dais.

A gift for the princess.

That cold chill I'd desired a minute ago had turned into an arctic freeze. A shudder wracked my body as the realization of what I was seeing finally hit me.

Someone did this *for* me. Someone sought Ruby out, drew her here where she was wanted for treason, and then murdered her without anyone noticing. Under all our noses. It was well known to those that mattered that Ruby and I weren't friends, but I'd caught a glimpse of the iron spikes nailing her body to the floor.

No one—not even Ruby—deserved to die like that.

I needed to call someone, tell someone. Yes. That was what I needed to do. I was about to turn to do just that when hard hands clamped around my shoulders and yanked, pulling me from the room and back into the hallway. Those same hands spun me before I even had the chance to kill the ball of light in my palm, so I caught his face before the light died.

Alistair.

"I didn't do it," I blurted, shock stealing all my sense. Could I sound any guiltier?

Alistair stared at me like I'd just gone off the deep end. "Of course you didn't. You weren't out of my sight for more than thirty seconds. I've heard stories of how lethal you are, but even you can't butcher a woman in that scant of time."

I couldn't put my finger on the "why," but relief stole through me at his staunch assuredness that I couldn't do that. Flashes of what I just saw blinked like strobe lights in my brain. The blood, the broken and tattered wings— or what was left of them—her naked body run through with spikes. I shuddered again, and this time, Alistair ran soothing hands down my arms. I was edging on hysteria in front of this poor man, and there was nothing I could do to stop it.

"We have to tell someone." I managed to choke out

before my eyes welled, and I covered my mouth before a sob could fall from my lips.

I'd seen horrible things in my life. I'd seen women butchered before. I saw Melody nearly cut in half. But I had someone to blame, had someone to punish. Now, my mind was still stuck on the shock of it, the sheer brutality of what was done to a woman I might not have liked, but sure as I was breathing, never wanted something like that for her.

"Barrett. I'll get Barrett. Or Marcus. Or my father. Fates, who am I supposed to go to, Alistair? Are there Ethereal police?"

Alistair continued to look at me like I'd lost my mind. Maybe I had. "The Keys are our… Think of them as investigators, like Scotland Yard, but regular citizens can't call them. They're in the employ of the Council. No. We need a friend here. The sooner, the better. This doesn't look good for us."

I didn't understand him at all. "Why? We didn't do anything. I just found her like that. I could never…"

"We're demons, Max. She was evidently an angel if those mauled wings are anything to go by. Unless we get someone to believe us and soon, we are about to be in the middle of a war."

No sooner were those words out of his mouth, was

the corridor flooded with people. And I quickly found out the hard way that Aether—or some offshoot of it—had a jail.

The cement slab under my ass might as well have been a glacier. Given my flimsy dress, I had nothing to protect me from the freezing stone, and no way to heat myself. The stone, the bars, the ceiling, everything was warded against magic. Runes of nulling were carved into nearly every inch of my cell, the magic of them grating against my skin worse than any sandpaper. Everything about myself, everything that made me who I was, seemed stripped, tattered, pulled from my very bones as I sat shivering in the silence. Even my innate demon magic seemed muted, muffled, ripped away. Alistair sat in an adjacent cell, his tuxedo jacket rumpled from the not-so-polite way we were hauled down here.

The only good thing I could say for the place was they didn't skimp on the security. A guard was posted outside both Alistair's and my cell, and we'd been forcefully requested not to speak. AKA, they slammed Alistair against the bars of his cell to shut him up when he'd only asked a question. I didn't want to know what someone had to do to get permanently remanded to one of these cells.

Footsteps echoed through my cell block, but I didn't look. This was the fifth time I'd heard steps coming my way, and every time I glanced up, the disappointment of no one coming for me tore me more.

"You sure know how to ruin a good party," a cultured British voice called to me, and I finally raised my eyes.

Barrett. Thank the Fates.

"Barrett! Please tell me you're here for us. I didn't—couldn't—do something like that. Not even to her."

He sighed, nearly touching the bars, but remembered what they could do and thought better of it. Instead, his hand fell on the knot of his tie, loosening the fabric from his neck. "How many times have you died preventing innocent deaths? It's up to a hundred and fifty by now, right? Sure. I totally believe you could kill someone like that."

I was a little too freaked out to fully catch the sarcasm. "Sarcasm is only funny if I'm not being drained of all my magic, Barrett. I'm going to need you to be as literal as possible right now."

"And that brings me to why I'm here. Macallan, unlock these cells. The Fates would like to speak to both of them."

"Sir?" Macallan didn't seem like he wanted to unlock

either cell, in fact, his expression said he'd like to conveniently lose the key.

Barrett narrowed his eyes. "Is there a problem?"

"They're demons, sir. An angel was killed, surely the Fates wouldn't want them released." Macallan was whispering, but I heard him all the same.

"I can promise you that neither Maxima Alcado nor Alistair Quinn has ever harmed a single angel in their lives. Just because you're prejudiced against demons, doesn't make them murderers. Things like facts and reason take part in convicting someone, Macallan, not blind propaganda and bullshit. Now, do you want me to tell the Fates why they had to wait, or are you going to open the fucking door?"

Reluctantly, Macallan opened my cell, but I waited for him to get out of the way before I walked through the opening. Once I was out, the relief of my magic coming back had me almost giddy, and I really looked at Macallan. Abnormally tall, probably close to seven feet or so, bulky in the extreme, barrel-chested with a trunk of a neck, his general demeanor screamed malice. But his face told another story altogether, it said fear, insecurity, not hatred.

He feared demons. Given some of us were right bastards, I couldn't blame him.

"Macallan, is it?" At his stiff nod, I continued, "The

stories about demons aren't true for all of us. We are protectors, punishers of the wicked. Some of our kind go a little crazy, but that's true for all Ethereals." I sniffed, catching his scent, the light of his magic telling me what kind of Ethereal he was. I knew what he was before the door opened, the runes unable to take that away from me at least. "You're a shifter. Plenty of your kind have turned, haven't they? But no one blames the whole for the actions of a few. We only ask for the same courtesy."

Macallan gave me another stiff nod. "Your Majesty, I know you are better than some. I heard about what you did to Finn Lorenson. You were within your rights to kill him, and you didn't, so I know there is good in you. But you might want to watch out who you spend time with." His eyes flashed to Alistair and back to me. "Not everyone has a reputation like yours."

I almost giggled. Did he mean Alistair had a shitty rep and mine was the good one? No fucking way.

"I'll keep that in mind."

Macallan nodded to the other guard whose name I didn't catch, and Alistair was freed. He didn't have the same hesitation I did about getting out of his cell. As soon as the door was cracked, Alistair bolted from the rune carved room. He also spat at the guard's boots as he left, the red-tinted saliva hitting the floor just shy of the guard. Alistair couldn't heal in the cell, so his mouth was still bleeding from the brutal shove against the bars.

Alistair squared up against the guard, looking like he'd rather throw a couple of punches rather than get the hell out of here.

"Hey, Knight?"

Alistair's body didn't move, but his glowing amber gaze slid from the guard to me.

"Want to get the fuck out of here before they figure out a way to make us stay? Get your shit together, and let's go."

His eyes narrowed in contempt, the animalistic growl rumbling from his throat made the hair on my arms stand on end. With a flash of fang, he took his leave of the guard and followed us down the almost never-ending corridor, up the stone steps to a set of heavily guarded double doors. We had less trouble with these guards. They opened the doors as if they were glad to see the backs of us, and then we were back in the sea of pulse-pounding music and writhing bodies.

I'd never been so happy to see the overcrowded club in my life. Barrett had to keep me steady when I nearly lost my feet in relief, but we never stopped moving. The Fates wanted to talk to us, and, dammit, I wanted to talk to them, too. They had to know who did this, didn't they?

Atropos cut the threads of life, right? That meant she had to know when someone died. Was it too far a stretch to think she'd also know how?

Barrett led us to an office I knew well. The brass "Management" plaque was familiar enough to ease my nerves a bit, until I remembered the last time I was here outside Caim's office—Ruby was, too. That thought brought flashes of the high courtroom painted with her blood through my brain with enough force to cause me to stumble again.

Before he opened the door, Barrett turned me to face him, his hands coming down on my shoulders. Whispered words I couldn't make out poured from his lips, and the lingering queasiness from the null wards fell away.

"Do not, under any circumstances, let them see you flinch, Maxima." Barrett's words were a fierce whisper of warning. "You are strong, you are capable, and they need to see you as such. You did nothing wrong, so don't let them see you think otherwise. Do you understand?"

At my nod, he released my shoulders, and I stood straight, pulling on a cloak of confidence I certainly didn't feel.

"And you," Barrett addressed Alistair, "keep your nose clean for five freaking minutes while Max talks her way out of this mess. Do you think you can do that, or am I going to have to send you back to the holding cell?"

Alistair seemed to want to argue, and that's just what he did.

"I want to be in there with her. I'm her alibi. I know she didn't do anything."

Barrett rolled his eyes. "No, Junior, I'm her alibi. Ruby was murdered hours ago when Max was with me. Speaking of, where were you between the hours of 4 p.m. and 8 p.m.?"

Alistair took a step back in affront. "In Hell. At my post." A growl escaped him—the same animalistic rumble that made all the hairs on my body stand on end.

"You'd better have been."

Barrett looped his arm with mine, pulled open the door, and dragged me through with him. I gave Alistair an apologetic glance before the door closed, but the expression I got back was nothing if not resolute. This wasn't the first time someone had slighted Alistair, and from the look on his face, it wouldn't be the last.

"What the *hell* was that about?" I leaned into Barrett and hissed.

"I'll tell you later. You have bigger fish to fry." Barrett kept his voice a whisper as he led me through the archway of books and into Caim's office.

The same three women I'd spent all day getting ready

to meet, the same ones I'd been presented to like a slab of beef, the same ones who thought my mother's blood was an affront, sat with their asses perched on the edge of Caim's desk, calm as you please.

Atropos, my brand-new nemesis spoke first, her words just about as damning as they could be. "You, my little princess, are in some deep shit."

I had a feeling she was right.

CHAPTER EIGHT

I'd wanted to be cool and collected. I'd wanted to handle this situation with the grace of my station. Wanted to show these three women—deities, gods, whatever—that I was fit to lead my people, to judge them. Instead, I was my regular sassy self and pissed people off.

Go figure.

"I'm in deep shit? Yeah, apparently, I've got a benefactor who thinks murder is an appropriate gift. I'd say the shit is about waist-high." My particular brand of cheek was not appreciated by this group. Barrett, to his credit, elbowed me in the side, but I ignored him. I was too busy staring at Atropos' face to see if she'd give anything away.

She didn't, so I continued, "You're supposed to be

the cutter of the thread, right? So why don't you tell us who did it? Because it sure as shit wasn't me, and it wasn't Alistair, either." I finished off my rant with a defiant crossing of my arms coupled with a hip jut. Yeah, it was a defensive posture, but screw it. If these women were trying to imply I had something to do with Ruby's murder, they were dead wrong.

But something passed over Atropos' face. It was a little bit of fear mixed with uncertainty and general malcontent. *Oh, this is worse than I thought.* As the silence lingered, my feeling of dread only grew.

Clotho huffed and pushed off the desk to pace the length of Caim's office. "We don't know who killed the angel." She broke the silence with *that* admission. Both Lachesis and Atropos seemed shocked she would say as much.

"But knowing that information is typical, correct?" I needed to clarify that point before it got lost in whatever they were about to hit me with.

Atropos snorted, rolling her eyes like the teenager she definitely was not. "Yes. Usually—as in every other death since the beginning of time—I've been able to see the causation and circumstances of death. Not only was this angel's thread cut, but it wasn't cut by me. Someone killed this woman right under my nose."

Which seemed like a kind of big thing for her to

admit, and also seemed like something I probably shouldn't know. Not if I wanted to keep breathing.

"So not only do I have a murdery benefactor, I have one that seems to know how to circumvent a Fate." I murmured this revelation to myself, but that didn't stop Atropos from narrowing her eyes at me.

"We know Max didn't do this." Barrett chimed in at my defense. "She was with me all day. In fact, Atropos herself made it so Max wouldn't be alone the entire evening with her 'don't turn a man down' shtick."

Glad I wasn't the only one who thought that edict was bullshit.

"If it weren't for the stasis spell cast on the body, maybe the timeline could be proven, but it can't," Lachesis countered. "We have no idea when Ruby Sinclair was murdered. It could have been six months ago for all we know."

I wanted to tell them how long I'd been searching for Ruby, how long I looked without even so much as a blip. If she'd been under a stasis spell, it was likely she'd been dead the whole time and brought out when it would be most convenient for her killer. I wanted to tell them, but I didn't. I had no illusions that the admission would make me seem more guilty and not less.

But they wanted to talk to me for a reason, and I was done catering to this merry-go-round of bullshit. "You ladies sprang me from jail, that must mean you want something. What is it?"

Atropos almost smiled at my blunt question. Almost, but not quite.

"We want you to find the murderer. Since it seems the act was presented as a gift to you, you are the person best to investigate it. We want you to resolve all of this. Immediately. You have forty-eight hours to bring the killer to us," she ordered in an airy way that told of eons of getting exactly what she wanted.

Was I supposed to fall on bended knee and do her bidding? It didn't matter if I was or wasn't supposed to, I wasn't gonna.

"Say what now? You want me to solve a murder you have no information on in less time than it takes to make good tamales. Or what?"

Atropos and Clotho seemed a little taken aback at my question, but Lachesis covered her face with her hand to hide her smile.

"What do you mean, or what?" Atropos asked.

"Exactly what I said. I have forty-eight hours, *or what*? Why shouldn't I just give you the middle finger and move on with my life? You know I didn't kill Ruby, because I've already prevented the war this would start twice already. You know I didn't kill her because if I had, not only would I not have bungled it in such a fashion, I sure as hell wouldn't have arranged the evidence to point right back at myself. Forty-eight hours. Or. What?" I demanded through gritted teeth.

Atropos' face turned an unhealthy shade of red, but honestly, I didn't give a ripe shit.

"How about if you don't find the murderer, we'll blame it on you. A demon killing an angel wouldn't go over too well, Armistice and all. Or maybe we'll blame your friend Alistair. Clotho has had it out for him for ages, I'm sure she wouldn't mind thrusting an entire war on his shoulders. Maybe we'll divvy it up between the two of you, really throw you under the bus."

I wanted to tell them they couldn't do that, but I knew better. They could and would. Out of spite, out of boredom.

"So the three of you have no honor whatsoever. Good to know. Anything you can add so I can find this bastard, or am I completely on my own?"

Atropos gave me a beatific smile. "You're on your own, Maxima. Don't fuck it up."

I was momentarily tempted to snap my fingers and light her and her sisters on fire, but Barrett snatched my elbow before I could act on my impulses.

"What in the fresh hell was that?" He dragged me from Caim's office back to the too-loud club, the thumping base and strobe lights only serving to fuel my anger.

"That was our bosses being assholes, Barrett. What part of that was unclear?"

Barrett's grip grew tighter, enough for me to know he meant business but not enough to really hurt. "You openly challenged the Fates, Maxima. Are you high, or do you have a death wish?"

He knew better than that. He knew exactly why I challenged them, and if he had less to lose, he would have, too.

"They were acting like scared bullies. Do I bow down to bullies, Barrett?" I didn't even give him a chance to answer. "No, I don't. I didn't bow down to Finn Lorenson this morning, and I'm sure as shit not going to bow down to three women who can't see the forest for the fucking trees. Not today, and not any other damn day."

Barrett pinched the bridge of his nose, dragging me away from the thumping music and down a semi-quiet hallway. I really didn't have time to deal with his judgment. Before I could tell Barrett just that, Alistair picked that moment of tense silence to appear out of thin freaking air and insert himself into the conversation.

"What happened? What did they say?"

How, exactly, did I explain that the Fates were trying

to blame it all on us? How did I explain that the forty-eight-hour deadline to find the real killer was a joke? That it was a way to get me to chase my tail long enough to screw me and mine over?

"I have forty-eight hours to find the killer."

He frowned, probably just like I did not five minutes ago when the Fates told me and asked the same damn question I did. "Or what?"

My laugh was bitter and a little hysterical, making Alistair's eyebrows crawl up his forehead. "Or they blame me, or you, or the both of us. Turns out they have no idea who did it, and now, it's my job to find out. Plus, we have to hope it wasn't another demon, or it's going to start the end of the world. Wish me luck, Knight, because I believe the both of us are just about fucked."

"Wha—" he began, but I cut him off. What part of the time limit thing did he not understand? Did he not comprehend just how short forty-eight hours was?

"Alistair, I don't have time to explain. The clock is ticking, and unless you say you killed an angel and my investigation is moot, I have a job to do."

With that, I gave him my back and addressed Barrett. "Where's Caim?"

Caim was the owner of Aether, an angel, held the angel seat of the Council, and was the keeper of the records. On top of that, he used to be Ruby's boss. If anyone knew anything about the circumstances of Ruby's death, it would be Caim.

Before Barrett could answer me, Alistair spun me to face him. Since I wasn't obligated to be nice anymore, I wasn't. A snap of my fingers had Alistair's arms involuntarily bound to his sides, his legs sticking together so he couldn't take a single step. Shock warped his face, which was supremely satisfying.

"What in the bloody hell did you do to me?" He seethed, flashing his fangs and amber eyes.

Interestingly enough, Alistair had upper and lower fangs, the second incisor and canine of both sets pointed, meaning eight razor-sharp teeth to fight with on top of who knew what else. They didn't look like wraith fangs or even the ones on Micah, the murdering incubus.

"I don't like being manhandled. Keep your hands to yourself, Knight, or I will remove the use of them altogether. Now what do you want?"

Alistair narrowed his eyes as if my spell was somehow an affront when he was the one who kept grabbing people. *Idiot.*

"You shouldn't be doing this alone. Or at all, for that matter. You know nothing of our world, Maxima. You're just a witch in a demon's body. You're going to get yourself killed."

"I wouldn't—" Barrett began, but I didn't let him warn Alistair.

No, this was a lesson the man needed to learn. And fast. Snapping my fingers again, I watched his lips mash together. I didn't remove them completely like I did with Ian that one time, but only because I wasn't nearly as mad.

Alistair didn't know me. He had no idea what I was capable of.

"This witch knew enough about our world to put down Samael, a demon that had been sowing doubt and contention for years. This witch destroyed one of the only ways on this plane to kill a demon. This witch has been on her own for a long fucking time. How about you don't tell me what I can and can't do?"

Alistair's irritated scream was muffled by his closed lips. Too late, buddy.

I turned back to Barrett. "Caim?"

"He's at our house."

I nodded and began walking down the hall toward the portal to Barrett's home.

"Are you going to let him out of that spell, or are you going to wait for one of the other witches to take pity on him?"

I debated the ramifications of Alistair being left helpless in a club full of witches on the verge of an orgy. Yeah, even I wasn't that cruel.

"Oh, fine. If you insist." I snapped my fingers once more, enjoying the thud of Alistair's body hitting the floor and the resulting string of curses flowing from his lips like tap water.

"There, I fixed it." I threaded my arm through Barrett's. "Now take me to Caim."

"Your thirst for revenge really scares the shit out of me. I hope you know that."

Me too, Barry. Me too.

CHAPTER NINE

To my ultimate irritation, I couldn't corner Caim the second I arrived with Barrett. Once we reached the sitting room, I quickly realized there was more than just Caim and Marcus waiting for us. The entire Council was there, perched on the available seating, sipping whichever brand of alcohol Barrett and Marcus kept in stock. I sincerely hoped they had a glass of Scotch with my name on it.

Marcus was the first to speak as he enveloped me in a hug. "Thank the Fates. I worried when Barrett told me you were taken to holding."

Holding? Is that what they called it? If that wasn't the entrance to Hell, I didn't know what it was.

"I'm fine. But I'd love to know what the hell is going

on. An update and a big glass of whiskey would be fabulous."

"I've got you covered." Barrett held three fingers in a cut crystal tumbler at my elbow.

"You are a prince among men. Did anyone ever tell you that?" I murmured before I tossed the burning liquid back in one swallow. It scalded my esophagus, but the warmth it brought made me feel whole for the first time since I was shoved into that cell.

"What did the Fates say to you, child?" Gorgon asked, his giant warlock's form folded into one of Barrett's leather club chairs. Gorgon was one of the few beings I would let get away with calling me a child. He meant no harm by it, and since he had probably lived a thousand lives, I had no problem with the moniker.

I swallowed air, wishing I had more whiskey. "I have forty-eight hours to solve this." I avoided the word murder solely for Caim's benefit. I didn't know how he felt about Ruby or her passing, but even I was scarred by what I'd seen. "If I don't bring Ruby's killer to the Fates in that time, they will blame her murder on me, Alistair Quinn, or the both of us. They don't seem too concerned that this will shatter the Armistice and start a war." In fact, it kind of seemed like Atropos would love to see me fail.

"Why can't they tell you who did it?" Caim's voice

was like broken glass and gravel. "Why are you looking into this and not them? Why…" Caim stood, and single-arm threw the closest bit of furniture into the wall. The chunky wood end table didn't stand a chance, shattering upon impact, the wood paneling of the wall cracking with the strain of the blow.

"They don't know who did it. Somehow, Ruby's thread was cut without Atropos knowing," Barrett answered for me since I was still staring at what used to be a solid piece of furniture.

I had questions for Caim, but I didn't know if I could ask them without him throwing something else.

"How could she not know who cut the thread?" Cinder, our resident dragon, asked in her thick Slavic accent. "No one in the history of forever has died without her knowing it. No one. Just like no one is born without Clotho knowing."

I walked to the wet bar and refilled my glass. No one lived without Clotho knowing, and no one died without Atropos knowing. Did that mean Lachesis knew all the rest? I wanted to ask, but I had a feeling Lachesis wouldn't answer me.

"And they want the youngest of us, the only demon, to investigate an angel's murder?" Caim scoffed. "If they don't know who cut her thread, how in the shit are you supposed to find out?"

He wasn't wrong, but I didn't have the time to let him rant. "You going to let me ask the things I need to ask? Or are you going to lose your shit again?"

Caim seemed to ponder my questions for a second before he feigned calm and took his seat. "Fire away."

I hesitated for a moment, waiting to see if he was actually holding his shit together, or if he'd lose it. He managed to fake his calm, so I began my interrogation.

"The Fates said Ruby was killed, but I thought angels and demons were the same in that they could be temporarily dead, but not permanently. Not without a special weapon. So, I guess what my question is—is how did Ruby die?"

Caim sucked in a breath, his eyes flashing golden, the same way Striker's did now that he'd come into his abilities. Caim was a hair's breadth away from losing what little composure he had, but still, he answered me.

"Typically, we are just as resilient as demons. But even we have ways to die. Whoever killed her did use a special weapon. The three spikes that nailed her to the floor are one of the few artifacts capable of rendering an angel powerless. Thank Perseus for that one."

"Perseus? You mean the demigod who killed Medusa, Perseus?"

"That's the one." Caim nodded before sipping from a

fresh refill of whiskey. "You see, Medusa was innocent. She was just going about her life, worshiping her chosen god, and then Poseidon comes along and rapes her in Athena's temple, right? Athena blames Medusa for defiling her temple, and curses her with snakes in her hair and a gaze that can turn a man to stone. Well, old Perseus needed Medusa's head for a weapon, so he snuck in her lair and cut her head off while she was sleeping, used the head to kill the monster, and everything was hunky-dory, right? No one ever says what happened after that. No one remembers that Medusa had two immortal sisters."

I had to admit the story of Perseus and Medusa always pissed me off. "The sisters killed him, didn't they?"

"Yup. Tortured him for a while, too. With iron spikes. Thirteen of them."

The mental image of a man impaled thirteen times made the whiskey in my belly want to come back up.

"Please tell me I don't have to go find ten more of those things."

"No. Just three more. Seven of them have been recovered over the years, held in a null room similar to our holding cells. The three used to murder Ruby will be heading there after they have been rendered inert."

I wondered if the person who killed Ruby had the

other three spikes. I wondered if those weapons were even something I could find.

"Okay, so I can try to find those spikes. Maybe the person who has the remaining three is either the person who killed Ruby or knows who did."

"That would be a dark path to take, child." Gorgon interrupted my musings. "Weapons like that have been outlawed since their creation. Anyone who has them in their possession isn't someone you want to cross. Spikes like those can kill more than just angels."

"Plus," Cinder added, "the Keys have been searching for forbidden weapons for ages. If they haven't found them, you are not likely to, either."

This was the second time I'd heard about the Keys tonight, and I still didn't fully understand who they were.

"The Keys are the Council's investigators, right?"

Cinder bowed her blonde head in a nod. "Correct. When they aren't investigating crimes, they search for forbidden weapons. We have been trying to prevent the violation of the Armistice for a very long time."

It made sense. No one wanted the angels and demons to go to war, especially not me, even if I didn't know what something like that might mean.

"So, I'm back to square one," I muttered.

Then I remembered the feather, the same one I'd

been using for the past six months to try and find Ruby. The same feather she'd dropped when I'd knocked her out of the tree in her Peregrine form. I now knew the spells I was using weren't completed because of the stasis-working Ruby was under. But now that it was lifted, it was possible I could use the feather as a beacon to find out where she'd been.

Maybe.

Okay, it was a long shot, but it seemed to be the only one I had.

Sighing, I raised my glass to the other Council members. "Less than twenty-four hours. To the shortest Council sitting in history." I tossed back the remaining whiskey. "I'm going home to pore over a grimoire or twelve. Call me if you guys have any info you want to share."

"We'll come by in a few hours to help." Barrett stood from his seat. "We need to wind the party down. Do you want me to tell your sister you went home?"

I wanted to tell him no, but I knew if I texted her, she wouldn't get it until she left. Electronics went wonky around the wards in this place.

"Sure. She's probably living it up, so don't cock-block her if you can help it. But if you see Della or Striker, send them my way, will you?"

With that, I took my leave of the Council and headed

back to Aether, so I could make my way home. With the wards around Barrett's home, I couldn't just snap my way out of there, and even if I could, I wouldn't. I let Barrett and Marcus have their privacy.

But when I stepped back into the corridor, I had a visitor waiting for me.

Andras stood leaning against the wall, his tuxedo bowtie undone, his hair in complete disarray.

"Please tell me you told those bitches where to go. Please tell me you turned them down."

He could only be referring to the three women I had no choice but to obey.

"It wasn't exactly like I had a choice. They said they would blame the whole thing on me and Alistair if I didn't. What the hell was I supposed to do? Say no?" I half-yelled, tossing my hands up. "I have forty-eight, no, I have less than that. I have less than two days to find out who killed Ruby. I wasn't afforded the luxury of a 'no.'"

Andras pushed off the wall and advanced on me. "They can't do this to you. To me, maybe, but not to you."

"They can, and they did. Now, I need to get home, search a spell book or two, and get cracking, because from what I hear, the Armistice is at stake. Yay on being half-demon. Glad that could come through for me in a clutch." I gave Andras a sarcastic double thumbs-up and skirted around him to the exit.

"You aren't doing this by yourself, Maxima. Not ever again. Not if I can help it."

I wanted to see his side, to think of him finally stepping up and being a dad. In fact, his words were kind in his own weird way. But they were too close to Alistair's, too close to another "you can't" instead of a "how can I help?" They were too close to Ian's rejection, to Aidan's protectiveness, to Cinder's warning.

Those words grated in the absolute worst way, and I turned back to face off against my dad.

Wouldn't be the first time.

"If you're just going to come in and take over, you can just stop right there. I don't need you to tell me what I can and can't do. I don't need you to tell me I'm ill-equipped to take this on. I know, trust me," I admitted with a mirthless chuckle. "But what I am not, is alone. I have a family I made all on my own, Andras, and at no point did that include you. You want to help? Fine. But get the fuck out of my way while you do it."

I gave him my back again, stomping down the corridor, and out of the obnoxiously loud club with too many people that all needed some damn clothes. The summer Denver air smacked me in the face, too hot, too dry, too something.

But I couldn't blame Denver, just like I couldn't blame the sun threatening to come up on the horizon.

I needed to get home, get changed, and get food. Then I was attacking this problem head-on.

Because it wasn't a question anymore of would or wouldn't I. It wasn't even a question of if I'd have help, or if I could bring the killer to the Fates.

It was more a question of what would happen when I did.

CHAPTER TEN

Walking down the sidewalk of a sleepy residential street at dawn would probably be normal enough if I weren't dressed in full presentation regalia—including the crown. My strappy shoes quietly clicked with each step as I walked the half-block from my brand-new snapping spot toward my house. This past winter, the ancient oaks that had shaded my front lawn—and hid my arrivals —fell during a freak ice storm.

I no longer felt comfortable just popping up on the exposed sidewalk in front of my house, so I picked a new spot down the street where the light didn't reach, and no one cared to look. A place where the oak trees converged in a canopy of leaves in between two stately properties, the houses almost angling away from one another. Neither family was in town that often, and the house across the street contained a crotchety blind man that was nice to his daughter, but an old bugger to everyone else. I paid attention to my neighbors, even if I made sure they didn't pay much attention to me.

My only hope was no one looked out their window to see me stalk home. My look-away spells only worked on my property, so if any of them saw me out here, I'd likely be the talk of our block's gossip hound, Mrs. Robicheaux. So far, I'd been off her radar, but my luck could only take me so far.

About three seconds into my trek, I realized I was being followed. Not because I heard footsteps, or because I could see anyone. Nope, that was for rookies.

I could feel eyes on me, sure as I was breathing, and I had to decide if I was going to glance over my shoulder or not. If I peered over my shoulder, I could no doubt see a glamour of some kind, but then I would give myself away. Then again, if I didn't look, then I couldn't tell how close they were, or if I could even defend myself, or if I should run. There were too many cons in the "not look" column. Not letting my steps falter, I inspected every darkened corner, allowing my eyes to lose focus on a few so I could maybe catch the shimmer of a cloaking spell out of the corner of my eye.

The faint webbing of light snagged my attention. Carefully hidden under the streetlamp across the street from my house, the hazy strands of the spell cloaked the figure of a man. Casually dressed in a T-shirt and jeans, he leaned against the lamppost with one shoulder, his ankles crossed, calm as you please. It was his lax stature that pissed me off.

"I know you're out there," I yelled loud enough for him to hear me, but I didn't tip my hand and look directly at him. "I can feel you staring at me. You have until I count to three to get off my street before I make you."

The man didn't even flinch as he nonchalantly plucked a stray piece of lint off his shirt before giving a jaw-cracking yawn.

"One." I began taking a step past him. "Two…" I never said three. Instead, I snapped my fingers, transporting myself directly behind him.

"I gave you until the count of three," I said in his ear, causing him to practically jump out of his skin.

The man whirled, surprise coloring his face as he looked me up and down. Too preoccupied with the fact that I could see him, he didn't notice my heel coming for his knee until it was too late. The sharp crack of his knee dislocating was louder than I thought it would be, but I refused to feel sorry for it. I also refused to feel an ounce of remorse for the left hook I aimed at his temple.

Well, until he blocked my fist.

But I'd been sparring with wolves all damn day followed by one of the most tedious, rage-inducing days of my life. I almost smiled at his gentle block before I seized his wrist, and then he was up and over my hip, and flat on his back on the ground in a move I'd been aching to use for ages. You could say what you wanted about this flimsy dress, but the abundance of slits sure made it easy to move. Before he could raise a hand to stop me, I had a knee in his neck, and my finger bore the green cast of my magic rising.

"You are not welcome, and no offense, buddy, but I gave you ample warning. So, you're going to tell me why you're here, or I'm going to make you cry for your mommy. Am I making myself clear?"

"Crystal," he wheezed, his air mostly cut off from my knee. His dark, coffee-colored eyes rolled back in his head.

I lifted some of my weight off of him, letting the man suck in a breath. "Why are you lurking outside my house?"

"I was sent to look out for you. It's dangerous times, Majesty."

So, he was a demon, but I knew that much already. He appeared fortyish, the faint creasing of laugh lines around his mouth and eyes telling his age, but his dark-brown hair was absent of any gray.

"By who?"

He seemed to think it over for a second until my knee made itself at home against his windpipe.

"Mister Quinn, Majesty," he croaked, his tan skin mottling to red.

I narrowed my eyes at him, and he elaborated, "Alistair Quinn."

At my growl, the man almost chuckled, or he would have if I hadn't been cutting off ninety percent of his air. I removed my knee from his neck, but since I didn't trust him at all, I whispered a word of binding and snapped my fingers. Incidentally, it was the same word of binding I'd used on his boss. His arms and legs snapped together as if bound in invisible ropes.

He seemed affronted at my lack of trust, but so far, Alistair Quinn had brought me nothing but irritation and a jail stint.

"You got a name?" I asked, mostly so I could stop calling him "the man" in my head.

"Ren, Majesty," he answered, causing my eye to twitch.

"Ren? Quit calling me 'Majesty.' It's irritating. Now, if I give you back the use of your legs, are you going to walk into my house without a fuss, or am I going to have to do something drastic?"

"No fuss from me, ma'am." Ren's smile was almost indulgent.

"Good." I snapped my fingers, letting him have the reins for half of his body.

Ren awkwardly stood, and we walked side by side toward my front door, the ward that surrounded the property only letting him pass once I put a hand on his shoulder and guided him through the webbed magic. Once inside, I escorted Ren to my kitchen.

"Have a seat." I waited until he relaxed as much as he was able, before snapping my fingers again and binding him to the chair. "No offense to you, but I need to change, and I can't have you snooping in my house. Add that to the fact that your boss is currently on my shit list, and well, you understand."

Ren gave me an exasperated sigh but didn't complain. I left him bound to the chair and raced upstairs, kicking off those stupid strappy shoes as I went. I was kinder to the dress, as delicate as it was, stripping it off and hanging it up, but the spiky crystal crown got a careless toss on top of my dresser. After I was clothed in jeans and a tank, and the makeup and blood were finally washed off my face, I padded back downstairs to raid the fridge.

There was a bunch of leftover pancakes in there from breakfast the morning before. Maria constantly scolded me for making so many, but I didn't see the need for not using up the entire box. Leftover pancakes were the best. I peeled the parchment paper off of four, popped them in the toaster, got out the butter, honey, and whipped cream, and set the table.

When they popped up, I dished two onto a plate for Ren, and then belatedly remembered to take him out of his binding.

"Breakfast?" I asked, passing over a napkin.

Ren narrowed his eyes at me.

"It's not poisoned," I said around a mouthful of hot pancakey goodness.

Ren carefully picked up his utensils and cut into the fluffy yumminess. His eyebrows did the talking for him as he tasted them. "This is good, Majesty."

"We talked about this. Majesty is not me. I was a Rogue for four hundred years, and I'm probably never going to like being in a position of authority. I'm just Max."

"You'll have to forgive me. I have been with the

Quinn family for many centuries, and they aren't as lax with their titles."

"You've been with the Quinn family? You mean, you work for them?"

Ren gave me an indulgent smile, the kind you give to kids when they're being adorable. I hated it.

"I'm a paladin. Think of us like butlers, only a touch more lethal. My family has been with the Quinn's since the beginning."

It kinda sounded like ownership, which made me bristle. "Like they own you?"

"No. Paladins live to serve. It is our purpose. We protect our charges, keep them on the straight and narrow. But no one owns us."

I calmed slightly. "And Alistair had you look out for me. Why?"

"He said a murder was committed at your presentation, and it was portrayed as a gift to you. He wanted me to make sure you arrived home safely."

So, Ren had the same information I did. But that wasn't exactly true. Ren knew a lot more about Alistair than I did.

"Tell me more about Alistair."

Ren swallowed before wiping his mouth with a napkin. "What do you wish to know?"

"Why Clotho hates him, for starters."

"Ah, yes. Clotho." Ren sighed. "Clotho hates the Quinn family as a whole, so I suppose she dislikes Alistair on principle. Several thousands of years ago, there was an arranged marriage that didn't go according to plan. It was supposed to bring the gaining family many children which Clotho foresaw, but the suitor from the Quinn family refused to go through with it. The union was never cemented, and the babies never born. Clotho has never forgiven the Quinns."

"So, someone didn't want to marry a person chosen for them. Makes perfect sense to me. I'd have probably done the same thing and likely flipped them off while I did it."

Ren chuckled. "The Quinn family is keen on irreverence. However, the offending party was cast out of the family, cut off, but still, Clotho refuses to forgive."

That explained why Clotho was pissed, but it didn't illuminate why the holding cell guard hated him. It honestly didn't explain much at all.

"I spoke to a man earlier today who said Alistair had a reputation. The way he spoke, it sounded unsavory—especially since apparently my rep is better than his. Care to elaborate?"

Ren huffed out an incredulous chuckle. "Unsavory? Unlikely. Mister Quinn is a Knight of Hell. His reputation is flawless. His brothers, his parents, his cousins?

Not so much. The Quinn family is known in some circles as..." He paused to search for the right word. "Infamous. In all matters. Alistair cleaves to the spirit of the law because that is what is expected of him and his station. His family, to the letter of it. Alistair is honorable but will make exceptions. The majority of the Quinns are not, but since they have followed the law to the letter, they can't be prosecuted. Add into that their high station, and well, few would go after them at all."

It surprised me that Ren was just offering up the information on a silver platter, and I asked him as much. "You are awfully forthcoming for a man I dropped on the sidewalk. Why cough up so much info?"

"You are our princess, Max. It would be like one of the humans snubbing the Queen of England. It just isn't done."

If that was the case, then I could ask really prying questions. The ones he probably didn't want to answer.

"If that's true, then tell me—did Alistair really send you to protect me, or did he want you as a spy?"

Ren winced, the answer clear on his face. Alistair sent his minion to spy on my house, and report back my comings and goings.

Red washed over my vision, my rage clouding every thought. Ren shoved himself back from the table, getting as far from me as he could in my small breakfast nook.

"I'm going to need to have a word with your boss," I ground out through gritted teeth.

Oh, I'd do more than have a *word* with Alistair. He wasn't going to know what hit him.

CHAPTER ELEVEN

"Maj—" Ren cut himself off. "*Miss*, I don't think Mister Quinn meant any harm in it. He only wanted to know if you left and who came to your home. I was supposed to guard you if you left the premises."

I felt the floor shake under my feet. "You mean he wanted to know when I got here, when I left, and who visited me. And that doesn't sound at all stalkery to you?"

"I was supposed to be under cloaking, hidden. Just to keep you safe."

What that really meant was Alistair didn't know I could see magics, didn't know I could see through glamours, and he wanted to keep his man under wraps. He wanted to spy on me and have me none the wiser.

High-handed, patriarchal, *motherfucker*.

"Ren, not only does that not make it any better, I'm having a very difficult time not ripping you limb from bloody limb where you stand. I suggest you leave. Do not come back to my house without an invitation from me, do you understand? There is no cloaking spell I can't detect, no glamour I can't see under. If you are here, I *will* know."

Ren nodded before falling to a knee. "I meant no offense, Majesty. I know you don't like to be called that, but you are what you are. I was under the impression you only wished not to see your guards, not that you didn't know I was there. It was only after you knocked me on my ass, did I realize you weren't in the loop. Please, just let me watch out for you. I won't report back to Mister Quinn."

Absolutely fucking not.

"You have been with the Quinns for how long? And I'm supposed to believe you'll do what I ask after meeting me for a half hour? I know my pancakes are fabulous, but even I'm not naïve enough to believe they can sow dissention that fast. No, you need to leave. Now."

Ren's face fell, his dark eyes turning sad, shame coloring his expression.

"As you wish, Majesty," Ren murmured, and I

watched him rise, stalk through my kitchen and out my front door.

I followed him, tracking his every step as he made his way down the pavement and to the sidewalk. Then I saw him disappear as the first rays of dawn reached the street.

One problem down.

Still seething, I went back inside my house, locking the door behind me, and stalked down to the basement. My casting room had gotten a workout in the past six months searching for Ruby. The spacious internal room had no windows and no electricity. The only modern thing it did have was an HVAC vent to combat the Colorado extremes of summer and winter. I was all for purity until it made me sweat. Snapping my fingers, all the candles in the room flared to life, their flames peaking high before dimming to a respectable flicker.

The drywall was covered in weathered wooden planks from the starboard side of a Spanish ship, *the* Spanish ship my mother and I boarded as we crossed the Atlantic in the 1600s. The *Corazon de Oro* only made two voyages—one to the Americas, and one back to Spain before it vanished from the ship logs. I had a feeling my mother had something to do with that, but I tracked pieces of the galleon down a few months ago. All that was left of her was on these walls, and something about the aged wood made me feel like I could do anything, could be anything.

On the east wall of the casting room was my altar, dried herbs, moon-charged crystals, several pillar candles of every color, an empty stone bowl, and my book. I hesitated to call it a grimoire. It was mostly a journal with a few spells thrown in.

No novice witch could follow it. Maria had tried some of my spells with little luck, and Maria was no apprentice. She'd said my spells didn't draw on the elements the way they should, and that was when we realized I wasn't like any witch that had ever been. I didn't draw on the earth or on fire. I didn't need a moon, or wind, or water. I only needed myself, and the demon power that coursed through my veins.

Somehow, I didn't think that was a good thing. It sounded like I was a necromancer, but the demon tethered was me. Maybe Aidan had been right those many months ago. Maybe his insult was the truth. Maybe I really was like all those damned witches who either served to do a demon's bidding, or tethered demons against their will and drew on their power until they were nothing more than husks.

Shoving those disparaging thoughts out of my mind, I considered what to do about Alistair. Should I just move on with my life, put solving Ruby's murder as my priority, and figure out how to get him back later? Or should I give in to the cloying need I felt to slap the shit out of the high-handed demon post haste?

Snatching a vial of salt from the apothecary cabinet on the south wall, I drew a large circle on the floor, my mind still whirling with the rage I felt. The sheer gall the man had to use one of his staff to spy on me. My whole body roiled with the need to bring Alistair to me, the need to draw him here, the need to trap him in a circle so I could teach him a lesson.

Once one end of the circle met the other, I capped the vial, sloppily returning it to the apothecary cabinet as I imagined slamming my fist into Alistair's aristocratic face.

It was no more than a thought, no words were spoken, no snapping fingers to signal my will, no incantations thought. Not a single Latin word passed my lips. Not that it had to be Latin to cast, it could be any language when used with intent.

But the earth still shook under my feet as if I'd cast a working, as if I was the one doing this. Wind whipped in a maelstrom in the closed room, the candles extinguishing with the gusts. Herbs and crystals fell to the floor, a few of the more fragile ones bursting into a thousand little pieces as they hit the ground. Burned out candles toppled from their stands, the pages of my book fluttering wildly.

A ring of green fire sprung up from the circle of salt, the flames waist-high as they danced to the tune of the wind. But they didn't spread throughout the room like a normal flame would. It was as if the magic of the closed circle kept them contained. And still, the earth roiled and pitched, nearly knocking me off my feet.

I had a sinking feeling this was me. All of this, the earth, the flames, the wind, was all me.

Before I could figure out how to make it all stop, a ball of black smoke formed in the center of the circle. It grew from the size of a baseball to the size of a cantaloupe in a matter of seconds. Then it bloomed, growing larger and larger until it coalesced into the shape of a man.

The smoke dissipated, leaving the crouched form of a man in the center of the flames. His tuxedo jacket smoldered, as if he'd run through an inferno. On the shoulder of his right side, the fabric was torn. Three crooked horns or spines seemed to have punched through the jacket, glowing fiery runes carved into the bone. Other glowing runes were etched into the blackened skin of his neck, his face, his hands. His entire right side was as if he was made of fire and soot. His hair, windswept and curling in the heat of him, seemed to be immersed in water. It floated in a nimbus cloud about his head defying gravity as if it were a personal affront.

But the left side of his face looked very familiar.

He stood from his crouch, first coming to his knees in a staggering move that made me realize that whatever I'd done, I'd hurt him. Glowing amber eyes burned with the same fire that lit the runes on his face, the lines seemingly etched in flames. But I knew that clenched jaw. I knew those lips. I knew that scowl.

Alistair.

"What have you done?" He seethed through gritted teeth, his hands clenched into fists at his sides.

I honestly didn't know, and I had exactly zero clue what I could tell him to explain the situation. What helped matters none at all was the fact that I was standing there completely dumbfounded, staring at the half-phased demon in the middle of my casting room.

"Play dumb all you want to, but you, Maxima, have royally fucked up. An Arcadios witch summoning a demon? You should have brushed up on your history, love. What you just did is a capital crime. As in, punishable by death."

Summoned a demon? Well, it was what I'd done even if I hadn't meant to. I didn't even know someone *could* summon a demon, let alone it was a punishable offense.

"But…" I trailed off, still completely shocked at the man standing in my casting circle. "I didn't summon you. I didn't—"

I couldn't even finish the sentence. What was I going to tell him? That I'd thought of punching him in the face and then he suddenly appeared? I'd manifested *things* before, but never *people*.

"You did. You pulled me across space and time. You pulled me not from this world, but from Hell, Maxima. You think that won't go unnoticed? You think after the stunt you pulled in Aether, I won't go directly to the Fates with this?"

I didn't even mean to do it, and the little shit was going to tattle on me?

"Maybe you will and maybe you won't. All I know is, I didn't mean to summon you. But you know what I didn't do? I didn't send a servant to spy on you. I didn't send a cloaked paladin to stand outside your home and report your comings and goings. Who did that?" I tapped my finger on my lips.

Shock creeped over Alistair's expression, followed by doubt. He didn't know if I was bluffing or not.

"I talked to your friend, Ren. Nice enough guy if he weren't perched outside my house. He didn't like it too much when I dislocated his knee, but since he's a demon serving the Quinns, well, I figure he'll heal."

Resolve colored his features. "And I'm supposed to believe you summoned me by accident? *Tsk, tsk, tsk,* Maxima. You are in deep trouble, Princess."

If he was right, if Arcadios witches were forbidden from summoning demons, then wasn't I in some deep shit? Would anyone believe that I'd done this by accident?

I had a feeling only one person might, but that meant making a call I did not want to make.

I needed Barrett.

CHAPTER TWELVE

I eyed my phone like a coiled snake. Calling Barrett was admitting defeat, guilt, and a whole host of other things I did not have the time or inclination to deal with. But with the summoned and bound demon in my basement, this was a problem I just couldn't ignore.

I hadn't taken a purse to Aether when I left to go spar with the wolves, so fortunately, I had my phone here. Unfortunately, I had about a zillion missed calls and texts, mostly from my father. Whoever gave him my phone number and taught that man how to text, deserved to be shot. I reluctantly went to Barrett's contact and hit the deceptively malicious "Call" button.

He answered on the second ring. "Hey, we're already

on our way, and I come bearing gifts of coffee and grimoires. And pastries. I think we cleaned out the entire case at that shop on Washburn. I almost feel sorry for their morning rush."

"Umm," I replied dumbly, unable to tell him the reason for my call. *Sack up, Maxima.* "I, umm, have a huge problem."

I got a beat of silence on the other end of the line, then the sound of an engine speeding up.

"What now?" Barrett's voice was knowingly accusatory. I didn't blame him. I kind of screwed up a lot.

Waffling for a moment on just how to word my current brush with stupidity, I stalled a bit too long for Barrett's liking.

"Maxima!"

"I accidentally summoned Alistair to my basement," I blurted, my words semi-garbled in their rush to fall from my mouth.

"You did what, now?" Barrett asked, genuinely confused.

My words were even more rushed than they were before, the story tumbling from my lips like boulders during a rockslide. "I accidentally summoned a demon. Alistair in particular, and he's currently stuck in a bound circle in my basement. And also, I have no idea how I did it. One second, I was thinking of punching him in the face while I was drawing a salt circle, and the next, he was in the middle of a circle in my casting room."

I heard a whole lot of nothing on the other end of the phone. Barrett either muted me, or he hung up. Suddenly, sounds were back, and Barrett's low, menacing voice reached me. "I will be at your house in two minutes. When I get there, I better not find what I think I'm going to. I'm going to pretend you didn't just tell me all that bullshit, and you fix it. Do you hear me, Maxima?" he threatened, hanging up on me.

Oh, I heard him all right. I just didn't have the first clue of how to do that. Not without either leaving a dead body or a witness behind.

Instead of trying to figure out how to kill Alistair and dispose of his body in the two minutes I had left, I called my little sister. Since it was way past dawn, and I had seen neither hide nor hair of her since pancakes the morning prior, my big sister concern-o-meter was pinging.

When her voicemail picked up, I said, "Ria, darling, I have every confidence you are getting laid good and proper and not lying in a ditch somewhere. But to ease my sisterly worry, call me back, nerd."

Maria didn't officially live here—her words—but she'd been staying here enough nights over the last six months that she had a room dedicated to her and her alone. Plus, after our mother left her to fend for herself against a Corax demon, well, let's just say Maria wasn't feeling all too keen to keep the status quo with Teresa. After living nearly four centuries with someone, Maria was also not too enthusiastic about living alone. I'd been happy to let her figure it out, and it wasn't like I didn't have the space.

I was tempted to call Striker, but since he'd been spending more time at Aether and not less, I knew he wouldn't pick up. I somehow doubted he'd be knee-deep in frolicking witches, but Striker had been reluctant to disclose what he was really doing in the nightclub that hid the doorways to so many pockets of the Ethereal.

I was going to be on my own to face Barrett's wrath, and it was probably for the best. When my two minutes were up, I opened my front door to see Barrett's Mercedes pull up. Marcus was driving, so at least no one was likely injured or maimed on their way here. Barrett slammed out of the two-door coupe, stalked up my front walk, and squared off with me on my front porch.

"Look, I didn't mean to do what I did." I desperately hoped he understood. "I don't know how I did it. Please, just help me fix it."

Barrett's eyes narrowed into a condemning scowl. "Take me to him."

I nodded and opened the door wide for him and Marcus—who was laden down with a drink tray full of coffees and two bags of what was likely pastry heaven, if the smell was anything to go by—to pass through the additional warding of my front door. I didn't say a word as I led them down the steps to my casting room. Even from the outside of the heavily warded room, I could hear Alistair railing colorful obscenities and promising vengeance.

When I opened the door, I got to see Alistair in all his furious glory, throwing himself against the walls of the circle. No matter how hard he pushed, he didn't seem to be able to break through the magics holding him there. Moreover, every time he threw himself against the wall of magic, his clothes came away smoldering, and his phase took over more and more of his body. The blackened skin of his phased half—or more than half now—crept across his face, the fiery runes glowing brighter. A pair of oddly angled horns jutted up from his head, peeking through the molten fire of his hair. It wasn't that they were jutting in weird directions, more that they were made of slate or some kind of stone instead of bone, chipped from time rather than sanded away.

"You actually did it. You really fucking did it," Barrett muttered to himself as the three of us watched Alistair toss his head back and let out an animalistic roar, his fangs sharp and gleaming against his charred skin.

And that was what his skin looked like: blackened like unspent charcoal. Like he was made from the sharp and pitted coals, and like he would burn just as bright.

Alistair's roar was loud enough and laced with enough power to cause the whole of my house to quake. I'd never been so happy I'd tuned my wards to muffle sound.

"Oh, knock it off," I yelled, causing Alistair to shut his trap for a bloody minute. "I was calling for help, no need to scream the house down."

Alistair bared his fangs at me like they would scare me. They would, they so totally would, but he didn't need to know that.

Barrett examined the circle for about two-point-five seconds before he reached for one of the coffees in Marcus' hands. "You have bourbon in here, right?"

I strode over to the apothecary cabinet and yanked open one of the lower drawers. Cracking open the bottle, I poured the bourbon into his cup until the liquid was nearly cresting the top. Barrett took a long pull before he dropped into the overstuffed chaise lounge in the corner.

"I have no bloody idea how you did that. There are no sigils drawn in the salt. There is no binding. There is nothing that tells me what kind of spell you used. There's nothing." He took another pull of his doctored coffee.

"You didn't use a spell at all, did you?" Marcus asked, and I shook my head.

"I swear, I just thought about punching him in his stupid face while I drew my salt circle. That's it. Then he just appeared."

Marcus frowned. "Why were you thinking of punching him?"

My smile was almost evil as I tattled on Alistair. "Because he had one of his paladins staked out in front of my house spying on me. Lucky for me, this douchebag didn't know I can see under glamours. By the way"—I turned to the douchebag in question—"Ren is plenty mad at you. He didn't like being used against his majesty."

Alistair flashed his fangs at me again. "What she is forgetting to mention, was that she summoned me from Hell. Not my house in New Orleans, not from this plane of existence. I was about to talk to someone important, and she ripped me from the bloody depths. I want out of this sodding prison, Maxima. Now."

I rolled my eyes. "What do you think I'm doing

here?" I half yelled, throwing my hands up in frustration. "I called my mentor, didn't I? I didn't murder you and dump your body in the freaking ocean—which is still on the table, by the way—so how about you settle the fuck down? You pacing and throwing yourself against the damn circle every five seconds isn't helping."

A menacingly quiet growl passed his lips.

"Yes, because growling at me is going to make me move faster."

"Wait a minute." Barrett seethed. "He had someone from his household staff watching you?"

I nodded. "But don't take my word for it, ask Stalker over here."

"Don't try to turn this around on me. Spying isn't against the law. Summoning is," Alistair shot back.

"Spying with intent to harm a member of the royal family is against the law, Alistair, and you know it." Marcus seethed. "So is attempting to infiltrate a Council member's home. Both charges are treason, in case you weren't aware. You know, punishable by death."

Alistair's expression turned mulish, his charred jaw set in a firm line. "So much for the position being open, huh? None of this matters. She's an Arcadios witch. No matter what you say, no matter what you do, an Arcadios witch summoned a demon." His chuckle was almost pitying. "It is of no consequence what I did first. She's still going to burn."

Burn? What would burning do? And then I got it. He meant in Hell in a place I couldn't escape. He meant torture, endless, excruciating torture. Forever.

"What I want to know is, why everyone is raising such a stink about Arcadios witches? What in the blue fuck did these bitches do to get on everyone's shit list?"

"You should know, you are one," Alistair shot back.

Wow. He really knew nothing about me whatsoever.

"All this talk about brushing up on *my* history, and you know not *one* fucking thing about me. I learned nothing from my coven. I was never inducted, never taught. Not one single spell. I learned everything I know today from research and pure dumb luck. My mother knew I was too powerful. From birth, she kept me hidden away because of what I am. So, fuck you very much, Alistair, I know exactly fuck all about this coven you vilify so much."

"But—"

"I was cast out at fourteen, you idiot. Do you know why? Because I came back from the dead after being burned at the stake. I know nothing about the Arcadios witches. And for the last damn time, I am not an Arcadios witch!"

Pinching the bridge of my nose, I realized the only

way I could get out of this—once I figured out how to get him safely out of the circle—was if he didn't remember it in the first place.

There was only one person I knew who could wipe someone's memory without blowback. It was time to call in my vampire assistant to pull my ass out of the fire.

CHAPTER THIRTEEN

This time, I did not make a phone call. I sent a text for my assistant-slash-grandma's assigned bodyguard to get her bloodsucking booty here pronto. Della was one of the few people who had keys to my place, the wards coded for her specifically. She couldn't walk someone in like Maria, or I could, but she could come as she pleased.

Last year, Della had saved my ass in a number of ways, first by streamlining my business when Striker had gone on his walkabout. The second, when she mesmerized my customers into getting the hell out of my shop when it was on fire. The added bonus of that, none of them had been the wiser that the fire happened in the first place. And third, when she'd gotten my shop back up and running, the building was rebuilt better than ever after the fire. Lately, the shop had been running smoothly without me, and I had to thank Della for that.

When I didn't get a text back, I called her, letting the phone ring until she finally picked up.

"You do know the shop doesn't open today, right?" she said thickly, her normally smooth French-Catalan accent rough with sleep.

"I kinda have a huge problem I need your help with."

Della groaned. "I'm still half-drunk. There is no way I'm driving. Can you make me a doorway?"

Della lived in my new-slash-old apartment above the shop, and luckily, making that door was one of the easier spells I knew. At least it was one of the few I couldn't fuck up.

"Sure, but don't freak out when you get here."

"*Quan sempre tinc?*" she asked in her native tongue. My Catalan was rusty, but I figured it was something like, "When have I ever?" or something close.

"Give me a minute, and I'll open a door in the living room. You don't have any midnight snacks there, right?"

By midnight snack, I meant humans. Della was a no-shit vampire, a species I thought was only relegated to fiction. I should have known better. All the other things were real—why wouldn't vampires be amongst us other freaks? But Della was one of the few vampires left on our plane. The way I heard it—and there wasn't too much written down about vampire lore in the first place—was that they left this plane and went to the Fae realm where they were more accepted. I didn't even know we had a Fae realm, and once that little tidbit fell out, I realized it was entirely possible to know too much, and I closed the door on investigating vamps.

Fairies had always freaked me way the hell out. Too many rules, and the accidentally owing them, and all the other shit I'd read in way too many Young Adult books. Nope. Hard pass.

"No, he went home after dinner." She giggled. "Get it? Because he was dinner."

I half-chuckled at her drunken joke. "I'm hanging up now. See you in a minute."

I ended the call and went back to the casting room, readying the ingredients for a doorway. Because I was at full strength—or more than full strength as I'd witnessed recently—I didn't need the blood of an animal or a wooden bowl of herbs. All I needed was a stick of chalk, a destination, and a whispered word of working.

But even that was too much.

Before I even said a word or thought of anything other than Della, as soon as the chalk was drawn, the portal opened into Della's apartment. The darkened living room lay just past the wall, a woman in a ball gown lay sprawled on the couch, the tulle of her dress pillowed in a mass of fabric frothing over the side of the furniture. I wanted to walk through the doorway, and the silvery break in the wall where the chalk used to be seemed stable enough, but I didn't trust it.

"Did you... did you guys see that?" I whispered, not taking my eyes off the brand-new doorway in my casting room.

"What kind of manifestation shit is this? You didn't do a spell at all. You didn't even snap your fingers." Marcus marveled behind me.

"I've seen you manifest objects before, Max." Barrett chimed in. "This is nothing like that."

I just shook my head. I had no more of a clue of what was going on than they did.

"Della?" I called, and my assistant sat up like a Jack-in-the-box.

She yawned an "I'm up" before she rubbed her eyes, making unintentional mascara raccoon rings. Della half-walked, half-staggered through the portal, making a zombie shuffle beeline to the coffee perched on the apothecary cabinet that I assumed she found by smell alone. She sucked back a healthy amount of caffeine before she noticed the pissed-off demon in the circle.

She frowned, shook her head, and then downed more

coffee, not saying a word until every drop of the brew was gone.

"I suppose the big problem is this." She gestured to Alistair. "Why do you have a demon in a circle? Isn't that frowned upon?"

Della herself frowned, and then swiped the last cup of coffee from the tray and plopped beside Barrett on the chaise. The carefully created up-do she'd had at the presentation was half-down in a mass of snarled curls. She also still had a bit of her midnight snack on the corner of her lips, the blood dried to a dark red that could have passed for smudged lipstick if I didn't know better.

I'd never seen the vampire less put together, but I supposed this was what I got for calling her at the ass end of dawn. The storybooks had it right; vampires were, in fact, nocturnal. Della just made do with daylight when she had to. Apparently, the myth that they burned in the sun was misinformation used to keep the zealots off their scent.

"Yes, this is the big problem, and I was hoping you could help me fix it. I was kinda hoping you could do that mesmerization mojo on him, so he forgets I accidentally summoned him."

Della snorted—which was unfortunate because she was drinking the last dregs of the final coffee. She coughed, sputtered, and let out the loudest cackle of all time. I swear, witches everywhere wished they had this kind of cackle.

"You know it doesn't work like that." She was still chuckling as she wiped her mouth.

I did not, in fact, know that. I knew exactly zero things about how that whole mind-melding forgetting mojo actually worked. "But all those people in the shop. You didn't use a spell or anything, you just looked at them funny, and they turned into lemmings."

Della gave me a wry smile. "Those were humans. Humans are easier to manipulate because they believe in magic. They believe in fairytales. Ethereals know better. Magic exists, but fairytales do not." She dropped that bit of wisdom on us and then gestured to Alistair. "Plus, he's a demon. His mind is likely too powerful for me to penetrate."

Alistair's menacing smile was almost smug. Add into that the fang he kept flashing, and he was becoming more and more irritating. At least he'd quit bellowing. For now.

Della was my last viable option for getting out of this the easy way. She was the only person I knew who could wipe someone's mind without side effects. But if Della couldn't help me—and as much as I liked my life as it was—I didn't want to mess with Alistair's mind. I'd seen it done too many times—Ethereals botching memory spells. It was too complicated and too delicate of work, and it almost always caused damage.

My remaining option seemed bleak. Alistair might not be the devil, but his shady ass was pretty close. And I was going to have to make a deal with him.

"Look, Knight, I have very few options here. The most drastic: I kill you and dump your body somewhere. You've been kind of a dick, but I doubt you deserve to die." I counted that option out on my finger. "The slightly less drastic: I perform a memory spell on you. Given that my magic seems to be going wonky, that would probably either turn you into a vegetable, or kill you, so I'm not a fan of that one. Then, shitty option number three." I continued counting. "I let you out and you tattle on me, which means I get deported to Hell and tortured for eternity. Also, not a fan of that one. So that leaves only one option."

Alistair's menacing smile turned practically malevolent. "You wish to make a deal with me."

"Bingo."

"You think I'm just going to let this go? You think I'm just going to stand here, and let you and your ilk carry on with your lives after you have dishonored me? You must be joking." He scoffed. "Do you know why Arcadios witches, in particular, are forbidden from summoning? Why demons will always look down on them? Why the Fates themselves were offended at you proudly displaying Arcadios blood? It seems your friends won't tell you, but make no mistake, Princess, I will."

"Don't," Marcus growled, his eyes flashing the iridescent blue of his wolf.

Alistair regarded the Alpha. "She deserves to know where she came from."

"Okay, Knight, spill it. Why is the coven who kicked me out for dying the worst ever?"

An expression passed over his face like something just dawned on him. "Your mother did you a favor. She excised you from a cesspool of corrupt witches that only thirsted for what they did not have. The Arcadios Coven was known for their necromancy, for their deals with demons in exchange for power. Centuries ago, it was a contract, a symbiotic relationship, a partnership. The demon lent power and life to the witch in exchange for service. But witches got greedy, and they started summoning and binding demons without consent. They drained them of all their power, turning them into no better than long-lived humans. Some were never heard from again."

So, the necromancer stories I'd heard—the reasons why it was so forbidden, the reasons it was illegal—was because the coven I'd come from abused their power.

"That says nothing of the children they sacrificed," Alistair added. "Did you know there actually is a special place in Hell for Arcadios witches? Your coven has its own wing."

"Does it matter to you at all that I didn't mean to summon you? Do you even care that I have no intention of binding you, draining you, or any other atrocity? Because I've had my will taken away." I suppressed a shudder. "I know how vile an act that is. I would never."

"But you did. And now you want to make a bargain. Have you ever dealt with a demon, Princess? The devil really is in the details."

"Oh, bloody hell, if you won't kill him, I will," Barrett muttered behind me.

But then it dawned on me, that was what he was bargaining for. His life.

"How about this? In exchange for not killing you and letting you out of this circle, you promise not to tell a single soul about my accidental summoning."

Alistair smiled, and then I added, "Also, you can't write, mime, sign, draw, or inform anyone in any way about the summoning. Ever."

His smile dimmed. "No deal."

I massaged my temples. "Ugh, why are you such a fucking prick?"

"It's a gift." He parroted my earlier words with a wry grin. "I require something for my mental anguish."

"What do you want, then? A pony?"

His expression sobered. "I want a favor. You owe me one for ripping me through the veil. That hurt, Maxima."

"Fine," I answered before I thought better of it, and if his expression was an indicator, I'd just royally screwed up.

CHAPTER FOURTEEN

"I want in on the investigation. I know more about this world than you do, and I could be of some help. That's not my favor. I want this from you as a courtesy since my name will get dragged through the mud right along with yours if you fail."

I pondered his request for a second before adding a stipulation of my own. "This favor can't get me into trouble, cause anyone's death, or harm anyone I care about. If any of those options are on the table, we can just squash all this, and I'll kill you right now."

Alistair sighed as if my distrust of him was taxing. "Of course."

"And no sexual favors," I added hastily.

He rolled his eyes and quipped, "I plan to earn those all on my own, thank you."

At his honest reply, my belly dipped. It was no secret Alistair was sexy as hell. The fact that he was half-phased and pissed off actually did little to deter my wayward libido. His scorched tuxedo jacket with the three spines punched through the shoulder, his half-open dress shirt that showed both his blackened phased side and his pale human form, the cut of his abdomen and chest, the runes carved into his flesh that glowed like embers. Yeah. He radiated power and abandon, and yet, somehow, he also exuded control.

If he'd quit being a complete dick, he could probably earn those sexual favors. Maybe. Granted, the odds of him not being a complete asshole for the length of time it would take to change my mind about him was pretty slim.

Still, the man was very nice to look at.

"Deal." I did my best not to let my voice wobble as I met his gaze.

"It's a deal then. Get me out of this infernal circle. Please." That "please" he tacked on at the end was more of an afterthought than anything else, but I let him have it.

All this might have been an accident, but I'd taken something big away from him. I'd hurt him. I could give Alistair the benefit of the doubt. At least on this one thing.

Still, I raised my eyebrow at him so he knew I wasn't having any of that demanding bullshit. I'd been pondering how to get Alistair out of the circle without hurting him, or me, or anyone else in the room. My only solid theory was to overload the circle.

To do that, I'd need to bleed.

Not exactly my favorite pastime, but if it got him out safely, well, I couldn't knock it. Heaving a sigh, I plucked my athame from the altar, debating on the best place to cut myself. I wasn't my mother, and I sure as hell didn't know the spell that could heal wounds in a matter of seconds.

Then I remembered the vampire in the room.

"Hey, Della?" I called over my shoulder. "If I cut myself, are you going to go bananas and bite me?"

I felt this was a legitimate question, but Della snorted in derision. "No offense, Max, but you're not my type. I prefer humans. Ethereals taste weird."

Super. With no other reason to stall, I put the athame blade side up in the palm of my hand, closed my fingers around it, and pulled. The white-hot agony of the knife slicing through my flesh didn't hit me all at once. No, the blade was so sharp, I didn't feel it until the rain of droplets hit the salt.

Gritting my teeth against the pain, I squeezed droplets of my blood on every few inches of the circle.

Once the revolution was complete, the floor beneath us began to quake. I felt the spell overloading, and the burn of it racing over my skin like a flash fire. Then the spell snapped, cracked, and fizzled out, the green fire dancing high before snuffing out altogether.

The room was bathed in darkness, and only when Barrett snapped his fingers, did the remaining upright candles flare to life. I wanted to be happy I managed to fix what I had broken, but I didn't feel right. I staggered through the now-defunct circle to the door, and I was through and out of the room before I heard anyone calling my name.

I felt sick, and it wasn't the blood still falling from my fingers. My head ached, my body felt like it had been put through a meat grinder, and my stomach felt like a bag of roiling snakes. I staggered to the basement bathroom, barely managing to flip up the seat before I lost my pancakes in the toilet. I heaved until there was nothing left, only noticing my hair being held back after the worst of it had passed.

A cool washcloth was laid over the back of my neck, and I appreciated whoever was thoughtful enough to think of it. The same person who held my hair back flushed the toilet for me, and if I wasn't so exhausted, I'd hug them. After I brushed my teeth.

When I had enough strength, I opened my eyes,

catching a glimpse of the blackness swirling away in the bowl. What the fuck?

I ripped the washcloth off my neck and wiped my mouth. It came away streaked with black.

"Backlash," a voice murmured behind me. *Alistair*.

"What?" I managed to look up to meet his eyes. It was a short trip since he was crouched behind me, but even that little bit was exhausting. He was back to his normal un-phased self, only his shirt was still half open, and his hair looked like it'd gone through a wind tunnel, the curls a riot of brownish-red corkscrews.

"You took the spell into yourself. You…" He trailed off, hesitating to say the words. "You stopped the spell from hurting me and hurt yourself instead. I never wanted that. I didn't ask for that." He seemed almost angry that I followed through with the break that freed him.

"Well, you said I hurt you in the summoning. Any chance we can call it even?" I joked, knowing his answer before he even opened his mouth.

"Of course not." He chuckled, shaking his head.

"I'm not dying, right? That would suck for you not to get your favor before I kicked the bucket."

Barrett elbowed Alistair out of the way, kicking him out of the bathroom altogether. "You're not dying, you just broke an enormous working in the dumbest—and likely only—way possible."

"Well, it's me, so you know, standard."

Barrett nodded with a raised eyebrow that meant he was judging me as he blew on his fingers. He rubbed the digits together as he blew on them, and I watched as his magic sparked. A blur of midnight motes swirled over his fingers, and then he touched my forehead with them. It felt as if I had been plunged in a cool swimming pool on a hot summer day.

The cold tendrils of Barrett's magic flowed through me, dousing the smoldering bits left over from my overloading the circle. My stomach unknotted, and I could take a deep breath again, my only discomfort the itch of my skin knitting back together on my palm.

I watched as the flesh closed, still mesmerized that such healing even existed.

"Thank you." I sighed, those two words inadequate to describe just how much I appreciated his help.

Barrett shrugged. "It was the best I could do. But your body still needs to finish healing on its own."

"I'm sorry I dragged you into this. I never meant for any of this to happen, Barrett, I hope you know that."

He stood, holding out a hand for me to take. "Yeah, I know that." He pulled me from the bathroom floor, watching me like a hawk while I washed my hands and rinsed my mouth. "Look, Marcus and I will pore over the grimoires. I need you to take a quick nap—just a couple of hours," he insisted when I began to protest. "You need your strength. We'll see what we can find out about the spikes."

Reluctantly, I agreed, letting Barrett lead me up to bed. But I didn't see Alistair, and Maria never came home.

After a three-hour nap and a cup of coffee, I checked on Barrett and Marcus. I felt marginally better than I did when I passed out, sprawled diagonally across my bed. Nevertheless, I managed to dress myself, brush my teeth, and put my hair in some semblance of order—even if my whole body ached while I did it.

The pair of them were poring over a crate full of ancient leather-bound grimoires, spread out over my entire living room. The couch, coffee table, and end tables were all filled with open books. Barrett's hair was a disheveled mess and Marcus looked ready to drop. Their expressions told the tale well enough. They had found exactly dick after their tireless searching.

"You guys need to get some rest." I startled Barrett enough for him to nearly fall off the couch.

Marcus didn't even glance up from his reading, his

brow puckered in concentration. "We have forty-two hours, kid. Rest can come later."

"Said the man who made me take a nap." I noted the blatant hypocrisy in his statement.

"*I* didn't just have a spell blowback on me. *I* wasn't throwing up black goo. Therefore, *I* can do whatever the hell I want," Marcus shot back.

I had to give it to him, he wasn't wrong.

"Touché. You guys find anything?" I asked, diverting his attention.

Barrett growled before slamming a giant grimoire shut. "No. All the lore on the spikes is either too vague or too specific to the ones we already found. There isn't even a hint of where the other spikes might be, what was done with them after Perseus was killed, or what became of the Gorgons after they managed to kill a demigod. And I'd ask Atropos, but she won't answer my calls."

Well, that didn't surprise me at all.

"Is that something she would know? How much do the three of them actually see?"

Barrett shrugged. "I have no idea. The Fates are a bit tight-lipped about their abilities outside of the spinning, drawing, and cutting stuff. I don't think she'd even answer me if I managed to get her to deign to talk to me.

She's probably still pissed at me for arguing for your release."

Surprise rocked through me.

"You argued for me?" My voice clogged with something I didn't want to name.

I didn't have too many people in my life who would argue with anyone for me, let alone the bloody Fates. Choking back tears, I carefully stepped over the ancient books to Barrett and attack-hugged him. He seemed surprised at my emotion, but I guessed he didn't understand. I'd been scarred by people abandoning me when times had gotten tough for the majority of my life. When I found a person willing to go to bat for me, I never let them go.

"Of course I did, hon," he whispered into my hair as he closed his arms around me to hug me back. "You can't get rid of me that easy, kid. I just started getting used to you."

Only a fourteen-hundred-year old witch could get away with calling me a kid.

I pulled back, wiping the tears off my face and sniffed. "Well, if she won't talk to you, I guess we need to pay her a visit. I need to inspect the crime scene, anyway. If we can't get clues from these books, maybe the killer left more than just a message behind."

But I didn't want to call Alistair. I didn't want to let

him in on the investigation. And I couldn't figure out if it was because I didn't trust him, or if I just didn't want to let myself.

Because the idea of letting Alistair in scared the shit out of me.

CHAPTER FIFTEEN

One would think that a nightclub would be barren at nine o'clock in the morning on a Monday, right? Not Aether. The weathered outside of the derelict warehouse didn't show it, but the inside of the witch club was teeming with people—most of them in various stages of undress. I felt sorely underdressed—or overdressed, as the case may be—in my black jeans, black tank, and—you guessed it—a pair of sweet black booties. My only nod to color was my blue hair and the tangle of assorted amulets hanging from my neck.

I wondered if these people had lives, or if since they lived so long, partying was all that they did. Or maybe since Aether was the hub of the community, this was where they did business.

Without clothes.

Barrett and Marcus went their own way to see if they could get an audience with one—or all three—of the Fates. I wouldn't begin to know how Barrett could call the Fates. Did they have cell phones? And if they weren't answering his calls, would they be more inclined to speak to him in person? I hoped they had more luck than I did. Somehow, I figured I would prefer looking at a crime scene to talking to Atropos again.

Luckily for me, the club wasn't nearly as packed near the entrance, letting me have an unobstructed beeline for the hallway I was after. Aether itself was a maze of corridors. Some doors led to storage rooms, and others led to different cities, a few even led to different planes of existence. Honestly, the door juju really freaked me out.

I suppose it would freak me out more if I couldn't see the magics surrounding them.

I was ten steps into the hallway that would take me to the high courtroom, when a familiar voice sounded behind me.

"I knew you'd leave me behind," Alistair playfully scolded, causing me to freeze and whirl to face him.

He was as casually dressed as I was, only he pulled it off way better than I did. Screw a tuxedo, this man shouldn't be without jeans and a black T-shirt. If he weren't such a dick all the time, I could definitely see myself drooling. Pity.

"Tough to exclude you when you bail all on your own. I didn't see you staying to help Barrett and Marcus search through the grimoires."

His smile was snide as he pushed off the wall he was leaning on. "I had a contact to get back to after I was so rudely interrupted. Sorry I couldn't stay to spin my wheels getting exactly nowhere."

I wondered how he knew we didn't find anything, but I almost didn't want to ask. Too bad my mouth couldn't help itself.

"How do you know we didn't break the case?" I asked accusingly as I crossed my arms.

"You wouldn't be here looking like you were on a mission if you did," he answered simply, and I couldn't argue.

"Fine, you really want to help? I'm not going to stop you. I need to look over the scene. See if I can get any clues."

"That's pretty much where I thought you'd go. I can't open the high courtroom door, so ladies first," he said gesturing for us to continue down the dark corridor toward the room in question.

Wait a minute.

"You can't open the door? Then how in the fuck

could you have…" I trailed off. "Atropos is a bitch and a half. Trying to blame you for something you couldn't have done."

Alistair sighed and kept walking. "Don't take this the wrong way, because I'm just spit-balling here, but couldn't the killer just use Ruby's hand to open the door? You know, like in one of those spy movies where they steal the eye for the retinal scan?"

I contemplated this for about a second.

"I'm not sure if the magic is still tuned to her. I figure not since she was wanted for treason, right? But if it was still tuned to her, then she'd have had to have been alive when she opened the door, wouldn't she?"

He shook his head, not in denial, more like he wasn't sure what the right answer was. When we reached the ominously inscribed door, I paused before touching the doorknob.

"In the interest of scientific theory, I would like you to try and open the door. Not because I don't trust you—because let's be real here, I don't—but because if I see you can't open it, then I am more inclined to believe what you say."

Alistair's eyes popped wide. "You don't like to beat around the bush at all, do you?"

"Honestly, I don't have that kind of time. I don't trust you. You think I'm an evil soul-sucking witch. I mean, if we know where each other stands, then we are more likely to get our ducks in a row. I have forty hours and some change to solve this shit, and even if I didn't, minced words aren't my forte." I gestured for him to try and open the door. "Have at it, Knight."

Alistair sighed heavily before giving me a look that couldn't be any more pointed if it were a sword. Reluctantly, his fingers closed over the doorknob. The smell of ozone was our only warning before a loud *zzzttt* sound echoed through the hallway, and Alistair was thrown back. His body hit the other side of the corridor before he landed on his hands and knees, panting.

"Holy. Shit," I muttered, trying not to laugh as faint tendrils of smoke wafted from his hair. "Are you okay?"

His expression was positively scathing as he slowly looked up at me. "No. I am not okay."

A giggle slipped out before I could stop it, and I slapped a hand over my mouth to contain the rest of the laughter that was bubbling up my throat.

"Do you want to try it? Maybe it will shock you, too."

Still chuckling, I remembered the time I blew up this door in particular with my powers. Yeah, even if I couldn't open this door, I could *so* open this door.

"Are you forgetting I was in here last night? I know I can open it—one way or another. Trust me."

"What's that supposed to mean?"

I shrugged before holding out a hand for him to grab. "I may have blown this door to smithereens last year." At his bewildered expression, I elaborated, "I was under the mistaken impression Barrett sent a demon to burn down my tattoo shop with me, my customers, and my artists inside so he could steal the demon blade. I was a little miffed."

Alistair's bewildered expression didn't cease after my explanation. "What?"

"That's a Fae-built door." He said it like that was supposed to mean something to me.

"I know." I shrugged again. "But I put it back together, so it's good as new."

"No, you don't understand. They are supposed to be impervious to tampering and indestructible."

"I know," I repeated. "Barrett said the same thing last year. It blew up easy enough, so I don't know what to tell you. Impervious and indestructible really aren't in my vocabulary."

"Neither is impossible," he muttered. "Well, go on then. If you're going to get zapped, I want to be here to see it."

I worried for about a second whether or not the door would attack me like it did Alistair before I yanked up my metaphorical big girl panties and gripped the doorknob. I didn't feel anything but cool metal. The knob turned easily in my hand just like it had the night before. Pushing open the heavy wooden door, I stared into the darkness.

A part of me didn't want to illuminate the room. I didn't want to see the blood and gore, but I didn't come all this way for nothing.

"*Detrahet me in lucem.*" I snapped my fingers once again in the gloom. A white ball of light bloomed in my palm, illuminating the area closest to me. But it wasn't enough.

Instead of looking for the likely nonexistent light switch, I tossed the ball of light up in the air, repeated the spell, and snapped with both hands. The ball exploded, washing the entire room in light just like when I'd been here before. Maybe that *was* the light switch.

"Good god, woman, you're a menace." Alistair covered his eyes. "Warn a guy, will you?"

But I didn't give a shit that I'd likely seared Alistair's retinas. I was too busy freaking the fuck out that there was nothing here. Not a speck of blood. Not a single crack in the marble where Ruby's body was nailed to the floor. Not one single shred of anything.

"What did they do? Where is everything? Why?" I sputtered, rage washing over me.

How was I supposed to figure out who killed Ruby if I couldn't find them? And how in the blue fuck was I supposed to find them if there wasn't a single thing I could use as a tracker?

"They took everything," Alistair muttered, aghast. "It's like they don't want you to find out who did it."

He spoke the exact words that just flashed like a neon sign in my brain. Maybe not the Fates, but someone didn't want me to find out who killed Ruby, and basic logic told me it was probably her killer. Which meant, her killer likely had access to this room.

A shudder racked my body. My only charitable thought was the fact that at least the killer couldn't possibly be Alistair. I'd need to check a few facts, but I highly doubted the killer could have used Ruby to open the door. After what she'd done, there was no way Barrett or Caim or even Marcus would allow her access.

No. The man who murdered Ruby could come and go through this room without injury. But rather than voice that uncharitable thought out loud, I kept it to myself. I'd ask Barrett later. If he had a leak—and this was a big fucking leak—then I wanted to help him stem it without prying eyes.

"He murdered a woman in this room. There has to be an imprint. I just have to find it."

"An imprint?" Alistair asked.

"Death leaves a mark on the earth the same way someone would notch a tree. Too many deaths and there is a spiritual groove scored in the earth. That's what makes ley lines. But every death—especially the brutal ones—leaves a stain."

"So, you would be able to see the murder then?"

I shook my head. "Maybe, maybe not. I've only done this once, and I was only able to see the point of death, and FYI, it wasn't pleasant."

I remembered the one and only time I searched for an imprint after a friend had passed under suspicious circumstances. I still remembered seeing Corrinne breathing her last breath as masculine hands choked the life out of her. If it weren't for the filigreed wedding band, I wouldn't have known who it was. Her husband said she'd drowned, and as the town magistrate, no one questioned him.

But I'd done much more than question him. And when the town magistrate had gone "missing," I'd been drowned in a lake for being a witch. Honestly, it was one of the less painful ways to go.

Alistair's hand on my shoulder made me jump, but when I refused to turn to look at him, he got in front of me and made me meet his eyes.

"What happened?" His voice was so soft, it made me want to answer him.

My smile was bitter. "A friend of mine died. I suspected the husband. I was right."

"No backlash, though, right?" He asked the question as if it mattered to him that I could end up hurting myself, and it finally made me realize I had absolutely no idea where I stood with him.

Did he give a shit? Did he think I was going to summon him in a circle again and drain the life out of him? Both? Neither?

Who the hell knew what was going on in that brain of his?

I shook my head. "No, but I was in a human house, not in a room made of magic. I make zero promises on what might happen."

I just hoped it ended a little better than the last time.

CHAPTER SIXTEEN

Eyeing the tracery magics in the room like they were coiled snakes, I bumped my slouchy satchel tote off my shoulder and started digging through it. I brought supplies with me like a good little witch. Maria would be so proud if she could see me right now. As many times as she'd scolded me for not being prepared, it made sense that the one time I was, she wasn't here to see it.

I made my way further into the never-ending room, stopping near the dais close to where I remembered Ruby laying. Kneeling, I started pulling out what I'd need: a candle, a small metal bowl, and a palm-sized vial of herbs and semi-dried flowers.

It was then that I noticed Alistair was still at the door and hadn't come any closer.

"What are you doing?" I asked. "Close the door and get over here. You saw the same thing I did last night, so I can use you."

Alistair's expression hadn't shifted one iota after he found out I'd blown up the door. Maybe I'd broken him?

"Yo, Knight, we're on kind of a time crunch here, so if you could get a move on that would be super helpful."

Alistair looked at me, looked at the door, and then back to me. "I'm not touching that bloody door again, Maxima. Did you forget I was shocked not five minutes ago? No, thank you."

I got up, stomped to the door, slammed it shut, and then tagged his wrist, dragging him to my pile of supplies.

"Sit," I insisted, resuming my kneel as I continued digging through my bag until I found my vial of salt.

"Good dog," he muttered, but relaxed into a kneel similar to mine.

I really wanted to roll my eyes, but I didn't want to give him the satisfaction of annoying me, which was no doubt his goal. Focusing on the task at hand, I lit the candle with a snap of my fingers. Alistair jumped when the candle flared to life, and that time, I did roll my eyes.

"Calm down. Aren't you fireproof?" I already knew the answer—the only demon who wasn't fireproof was me.

"Yes, but with you, one never knows."

He had a point, so I kept silent as I dumped the herbs and dried flowers into the bowl. The scent of the lemongrass, sage, rose, and lavender wafted up as I sprinkled salt into the basin, and snapped my fingers again to set it on fire. At least this time Alistair didn't jump.

Beginning in an almost inaudible chant, I muttered the same words I had when I was twenty-four and lost the first person to ever show me a bit of kindness. "*Ostende mihi vitae labe cito sublatus est. Mortis signum ad revelare.*"

Show me the stain of life that was taken too soon. Reveal the mark of death.

I'd repeated myself twice before Alistair chimed in and broke my concentration.

"Why is it you witches always use Latin? You sound like you're trying to raise the dead."

"A, you are not helping. B, it doesn't have to be Latin, it's just what I'm most comfortable using because that was the language all the grimoires I started out reading were written in. It could be any language if it is used with intent. I've used French Creole, English, Catalan, Norwegian, Arabic, Tagalog, and Cantonese, but I understand Latin- or Germanic-based languages better because they are my first languages. Any other observations you want to make, because I have to concentrate."

His expression was almost sheepish, so I let it go.

"Give me your hands. It'll be easier for you to not interrupt me if you can feel the magic." I grabbed his hands, crossing them wrist over wrist.

He started again before relaxing, the warmth of him seeping into my chilled fingers. I held his giant hands loosely so my rings didn't bite into his flesh, but it didn't matter how lax my grip was, I could feel the jolt of power under his flesh.

Closing my eyes, I began my chanting again, letting the power of our joined energies flow back and forth between us like an infinity loop of light. With each revolution of the spell, the loop spun faster and faster until it spun into a bright ball of light in my mind. A chill fell over me, and I reluctantly opened my eyes again, knowing that the working was done.

I let Alistair's hands go and stood, staring at my new view. The room as it was five minutes ago was still there, but a diaphanous overlay of Ruby's last moments played out on the marble clear as crystal.

Ruby's breath was labored, her chest rising and falling in faint little pants, and she gritted her teeth against the agony of the spike in her chest. Her formerly silky blonde hair was matted to her head in spots. In others, the corn-silk strands were dyed red with her own blood. Mascara smudged under her eyes, she silently wept as her breaths came faster. I couldn't hear them, but I knew they probably sounded wet with the blood that stained her lips.

A silvery spike etched with runes protruded from her crossed feet, a twin to the one lodged just to the right of her heart. It was as if the spikes weren't meant to kill her, but meant to bring the ultimate pain until her body gave out on her. Blood pooled underneath her body, either from the mangled wings ripped from her back, or from the spike nailing her to the marble.

A hooded man knelt over her, one hand in the pool of blood as if he'd like to paint with it, and the other holding another spike. He leaned close to her face, and an amulet swung out of his cloak toward her. Weakly, she grabbed it, but something in her expression changed once her fingers closed over the metal. With her last vestiges of strength, she ripped the necklace from his neck, a snide expression on her face as she spit blood at the cloaked man. We couldn't see where it landed because of the darkness of the cloak, but for Ruby's sake, I hoped it hit the mark.

The hand that was once in the pool of blood cracked across her cheek, and Ruby's fingers went slack, the amulet slipping from her grasp. The circle of metal rolled to a stop a few feet away from her outstretched fingers, but the man paid it no mind. He gathered her wrists together over her head and rammed the spike through both of her palms. Then, he pulled a mallet from beneath the billows of fabric, hammering the spike through her flesh and into the marble.

I wanted to look at the amulet, needing to study it, but I couldn't deny the pull I felt to watch Ruby's last breaths. Somehow, I felt like I owed it to her, to witness this terrible evil done to this flawed angel. I may have hated Ruby, I may have wanted her to pay for what she'd done, but not this way.

No one deserved this.

The man stood and watched as Ruby gasped once, twice, and then went still, her face going slack. The rigidness of pain left her body, and I knew her life was really and truly snuffed out.

Only then did I look at the amulet. Only then did I kneel to inspect the round disk of bronze carved with a symbol I'd seen before. In fact, I'd seen it yesterday.

On Finn's neck.

"I have a lead," I whispered as I watched the cloaked man pick up the amulet, wipe the blood off of it, and slip it around his wrist.

"You damn well better have a lead after making me watch that. This guy makes the torturers in Hell look like my nana's knitting circle." Alistair's hushed voice almost made me smile.

Almost, because the vision of Ruby's death wasn't over, and wouldn't be until her spirit left her body.

So, I watched some more and waited, owing it to Ruby to see everything I could. The cloaked man stood by, too, only he wasn't waiting exactly. No, he was performing a ritual, bathing a small dagger in Ruby's blood, then plucking a feather from one of her ruined wings, and binding it along with the amulet to the bloody knife with twine. Then, just as suddenly as he rammed the spike in her hands, he plunged the dagger in Ruby's heart.

As soon as the blade made contact, Ruby's eyes opened wide, blazing with pure light. Then just as quickly, her light snuffed out, flowing from her body into the amulet. The amulet glowed for one brief second before it faded, and then the whole scene died.

"Holy shit," Alistair murmured.

Holy shit was right. I knew Ruby's death was gruesome, but had I known it was that bad, I didn't know if I would have had the courage to do the spell in the first place. A chill rolled through my whole body, and I shuddered at the wash of cold.

"You said you had a lead. What was it?" Alistair asked, but I didn't know if I could answer him.

Finn was in Marcus' pack. Didn't I need his approval? Would he give it on my word alone? And could I even question someone without his consent? Questions roiled in my brain, and I wished I had someone to talk this out with. Someone I trusted.

I wanted Striker. Or Maria. Barrett. Hell, I'd take Aidan at this point. For a split second, I thought it was funny that when I listed all the people I trusted, Ian didn't make the cut. A year ago, he would have been at the top of the list, but now I'd take the BFF who betrayed me, the sister who left me behind, or the former trainer who would rather I not subject his brother to my particular brand of trouble.

I'd take all of those over the man who left me in the dust. Funny how abandonment worked.

"Tell me, Maxima. What was the lead?" Alistair asked me, but it was less a question and more of a demand.

"I don't know if I can." I did my best not to look like a whiny teenager and bite my lower lip.

"What in the bloody hell does that mean? It was the amulet, wasn't it? You've seen it before, haven't you?"

Dammit, why did the man have to be so freaking perceptive?

"Maybe? It looks like an amulet I saw yesterday, but if I go question the guy who had it, it could cause some heavy tension, so I'm trying to be an adult and figure out what the fuck to do, okay?"

Alistair just blinked at me. "You're actively trying *not* to cause trouble? I thought trouble was your middle name."

More like it followed me like a lost puppy.

"Look, I need to make a phone call before we go question this guy," I said while I drenched the embers of the herbs with a dousing spell before packing them and the candle back into my bag. "Let's get out of here so I can get reception, and when I make my call, mind your business. I'm not looking to start a new war while we're trying to prevent the one already looming over us."

Alistair raised his hands in surrender, but I did notice he didn't answer me one way or the other.

Once we were out of the high courtroom and in a spot with a tiny bit of reception, I called Marcus. When he didn't answer, I called him again. And again. I called Barrett, too. As well as Caim, and Cinder. Gorgon didn't have a phone, but if he would have had one, I probably would have called him, too. No one was answering.

Growling, I dialed Marcus one more time, this time actually leaving a voicemail, which I considered akin to torture.

Before the voicemail picked up, I put a deafness spell

on Alistair. Not my finest moment, but he didn't need to hear this.

"This is Marcus. Leave a message," the recording ordered in a tone that I'd never heard come out of Marcus' mouth. I did not have a good feeling about this at all.

"Marcus? Yeah, hi. It's Max. Look, I did a spell in the high courtroom that showed me Ruby's murder. I had to do the spell because someone had the entire room cleaned, and anyway, I saw an amulet the killer was wearing, and it looked like the one I ripped off of Finn yesterday. I'm going to the pack house to question him, so please don't kill me when you get there. I love you!" I hung up, managing to say all of that in one breath, the verbal diarrhea spewing freely.

Marcus was going to kill me.

I turned back to Alistair and remembered to lift the deafness from his ears. When the sound turned back on, he automatically seemed to know it was me, giving me a glare that could singe the surface of the sun.

"What?" I shrugged with a defensive stare. "Trust is earned."

Alistair crossed the few feet that separated us, getting right into my space. His blue eyes blazed golden as his demon peeked from his depths. "Yes, trust is earned, Princess. How exactly is a man supposed to earn your trust if you refuse to give him even an ounce of leeway to prove himself?"

I didn't have an answer for him. I wasn't sure if I ever would.

He remained in my space, still waiting for an answer to his question. Like a dog with a bone, he really didn't want to let this go. I couldn't answer him, and because I was a master at avoidance, I changed the subject.

"Look, we're about to do something highly stupid, and I need you to get on board, because this is going to suck in the extreme if you're not with me on this." Why I decided to lead with that, I had no idea, but I continued, not letting Alistair's searing expression hinder me. "Yesterday, I was attacked by a werewolf. Well, it was more like he charged me, and I didn't back down. Anyway, that werewolf had an amulet around his neck that looked very similar to the one we saw—"

"You're going to just blow right by what I said, aren't you? You're going to ignore the whole bit like I didn't even speak."

I heaved a sigh and forced myself to meet Alistair's gaze. The gold had receded, which made what I was about to say only slightly less painful. "I'm not a good bet, okay? I'm always going to be too something. Too loud, too rude, too whatever. You might like what you see now, but you'll change your mind. Everyone does.

Every single person I've ever cared about has left me behind in one way or another. You will too. You'd be better off picking someone else to mess around with."

Every single word out of my mouth was the truth, and I could tell he knew it as well when he took a step back. Even though I was the one doing the pushing, it still stung.

"You would rather do the leaving, then?" he asked like he knew the burn of being left behind, like he knew the exquisite sting of always being the one no one wanted to keep.

I shrugged, swallowing past the lump in my throat, and if my eyes were a bit wet, well, that was just the light. "It hurts a whole lot less when I'm not the one being left."

Gritting my teeth, I forced my tears back, stuffing that bit of pain that bubbled up to the surface back down to the depths of me. Why it made itself known was a mystery I didn't have time to crack.

I wanted to get Ruby's murder solved. I wanted to get out from under the Fates thumb. I wanted the threat of war in my rearview.

And I wanted the quiet burn in my chest whenever I thought of Alistair to go away. The only way to do that was to get him the hell out of my life.

"So, you want to go question a werewolf or what?"

CHAPTER SEVENTEEN

I eyed the guard to the dungeons—the same man who was barring my way, keeping me from questioning Finn. Honestly, I didn't blame him. I wasn't a shifter of any kind, so I shouldn't even be here. Plus, in no way did I have permission from his Alpha to enter these dungeons in the first place.

I knew it. He knew it. Hell, even Alistair knew it. The demon in question appeared as nonthreatening as a man that size could be, his hands stuffed in his pockets as he hovered to my right—behind me, but ready to fight if he needed to. Alistair didn't like being put in the back seat, but it had to be done.

But still, I needed to get past the guard, and I didn't want to resort to violence if I didn't have to. Especially since the guard in question had been a real stand-up guy when we sparred the day prior. His name was Hideyo, and if I remembered right, he was a Kitsuné. Hideyo didn't shift when we fought, but I'd heard the other shifters whisper about him. I'd never come across a Kitsuné in my travels, but I'd heard enough about them to know the phrase "sly like a fox" was their *modus operandi*.

"You know better than to ask me for passage, Max," Hideyo warned, the ancient spear in his hand at odds with his garb of black tactical pants, tight T-shirt, and gun belt. Likely, the spear was ceremonial, but I had no doubt he could use it if he needed to.

I sighed, not wanting to go through the entire spiel, but I needed to give the man something. "I'm trying really hard not to start shit here. You know about the angel that was murdered, right?" At his chin jut in the affirmative, I continued, "Well, I have to investigate her murder because the Fates decided to be dicks by putting me in charge and gave me a time limit. I have a feeling Finn knows something, although I seriously doubt he was involved since he's been locked up. I would really like to question him without violence or bloodshed, but honestly, I don't have the kind of time for diplomacy, so I'll shed it if I have to."

It was a threat wrapped in an explanation, but Hideyo caught it well enough. His face was the same picture of immovable stone he used right before he took someone down. I'd seen that expression first-hand before he landed me on my ass.

"Please keep in mind, I'm trying to be nice here. If I had the time to give the proper respect and go through the correct channels, I would. But I don't. So, pretty please with sugar on top, don't make me make you." I gently reminded him that I did, in fact, win our sparring session when I finally stopped trying to be nice.

"Fine, but if Marcus asks, you made me, deal?" Hideyo gave me a devious smile, tipping up his lips.

"Can do," I promised, and he stepped aside, giving us passage to the dank stairwell that led down to the cold sub-basement cells.

"And Max?" Hideyo called to my back after we'd taken several steps down. "Finn wasn't in these cells the whole time. We caught him trying to get a witch to reverse your curse."

My eye twitched at the word, and I wanted to argue that what I did to Finn wasn't a curse. It was punishment for being a sadistic prick, but I kept my mouth shut on that sticking point.

"Good to know. Thank you." I watched Hideyo's face for censure.

It was totally possible that not everyone agreed with what I did to Finn. Many shifters might think turning off their link to their animal was akin to death itself, only more drawn out. I'd considered that only after I judged Finn, but I couldn't lift the spell now, especially since he'd already tried to have someone remove it. Not unless I wanted to kill him.

The stone stairwell curved west the farther we descended, the walls practically weeping moisture the farther below ground we traveled. Even if I didn't already know we weren't in Colorado anymore, the wet sandstone walls would have been a big clue. Torches lit the arched ceilings, highlighting the fact that ninety-nine percent of the cells were empty.

That made total sense if you knew anything about shifters. They valued honesty and loyalty, even the ones who were considered shifty like the big cats and foxes. And to disobey an Alpha like Finn had done was usually met with a death sentence.

It was a hard way to live, but the togetherness in shifter clans made up for it. It was a promise to never be left behind, and Finn had taken his good fortune at finding a family and squandered it. Then, evidently, he'd taken it one step further by shirking his punishment. The fact that he wasn't already dead was likely a consideration Marcus had given to me, and I wondered why he didn't say anything about Finn last night.

But then I remembered the shitshow of epic proportions that was last night and gave him the benefit of the doubt.

The very last cell at the very end of a row of emptiness housed the pacing wolf. Or former wolf as the case may be. As soon as Finn saw me, he charged the bars—bars meant for wolves, shifters with immense strength and speed—and reached through them to grab at me. Human strength and speed or not, Finn was still fast and deadly enough to be a threat. His rough fingers grazed the front of my shirt before Alistair banded an arm around my middle and dragged me back out of Finn's reach.

"You stupid bitch." Finn seethed, his screams echoing off the stone walls. "I ought to rip you apart. I should rend you flesh from bone—"

Muttering under my breath, I twisted my hand like I was turning a key, cutting off his voice like turning off a faucet. Locking Finn away from his animal was my only option aside from killing him outright, but maybe I was too generous with my judgment. But turning off his voice did nothing but make his anger burn brighter. His mouth moved with the words he wished to scream at me, I just had the added benefit of not hearing them.

"While I suppose that spell is handy, cutting off his voice will hinder the questioning a bit. You have an idea of how we can get his attention?" Alistair whispered his question in my ear.

That's when I realized his arm hadn't moved from my waist, and the heat of him was still at my back. Everything in me clenched for one hot second before I stiffened and stepped away from him. But that step took way more willpower than I thought it would.

"Thanks." I referred to his save, glad my voice didn't sound as breathy as it felt. "I can get him to talk to me, I was just trying for the least amount of bloodshed. Jokes on me, right?"

With a bit of concentration, I could get Finn's attention easily enough. I focused on his body, letting the weight of it coalesce in my mind. Then it was as easy as flicking my fingers to throw him into the dank stone wall. His whole body thudded against the rough surface, his head especially giving a solid thwack.

Attention achieved.

The bitch of it was holding him there, but I wouldn't let that stop me.

"Finn, I need to talk to you, so I'm going to need you to put away your idiot bullshit for a few minutes. Can you do that for me?" I asked sweetly, even though I could feel the sweat on my brow from holding a nearly three-hundred-pound giant against a wall with my mind.

Finn's eyes narrowed, and he gave me a little nod. I

must have knocked some sense into him after all. Lucky me. But I wasn't a complete idiot, so I gave him his voice back, but kept him dangling from the wall with my mind. Finn, to his credit, kept his mouth shut.

Smart man.

"An angel was murdered last night, Finn." Fear crossed over his face, so I dissuaded the idea that I was here to blame him. "Now, I'm not stupid enough to think you killed her. For one, you're not smart enough to pull off something that clever, and two, the guy was closer to my size than yours. But the murderer had an amulet like yours, and I want to know everything there is to know about that necklace."

He gave me a hesitant little nod, and I gave him control over his body, letting him loose from my mental grip. Finn landed on the stone floor with a thump, but he kept his feet. The release of him caused my whole body to sag in relief. Doing shit the nice way was hard.

"You mean the necklace you ripped off my neck yesterday?" His voice was cold, bitterness leaking into every syllable, but I let it go.

"The very one." I nodded as I willed my body not to give out on me. Telekinetic spells weren't made for the weak.

"It's the Nordic rune for protection." He pulled the bronze disk from his pocket, the attached necklace's clasp still broken from when I'd yanked it. "My mother gave it to me when I left our pack at sixteen. Did you know what it was when you ripped it from my neck?"

"No. Honestly? It was waving in my face, and I was pissed off. It wouldn't have stopped me from doing what I did, Finn. Your punishment is not a curse. It's a chance for you to see what it's like to be weak, so you understand that it is your job to protect. Well, that, and to teach you that being a prick doesn't pay."

If I were being really honest, I just didn't want to kill him, and that's precisely what would have happened if I didn't punish Finn.

His attention was on the circle of metal in his palm. My focus was on Finn. So when Marcus' voice came from behind me, I nearly jumped out of my skin.

"What the fuck are you doing, Maxima?"

His voice had that low, growly quality that gave me a chill of fear. So far, I'd never really seen Marcus pissed. Miffed at a push, but never blisteringly angry and especially not at me. His eyes blazed the blue of his wolf, and all I wanted to do was cower behind Alistair.

I'd also forgotten just how big Marcus was. Barrett was six feet, but Marcus was a burly six foot four with shoulders wide enough to make you wonder if he could pass through a doorway without trouble.

"I'm questioning Finn," I answered meekly, and meek was never a word I associated with myself.

"In my home? Without my consent?" Marcus seemed calm, but I had no illusions he was anything other than murderous. I caught a glimpse of Barrett right behind him, and the "oh, shit" expression on his face did nothing to help my nerves.

"Yes? You didn't check your voicemail, did you? I tried calling you. And Barrett. And every other Council member. No one answered."

Marcus' scowl deepened.

"I swear, if I weren't under the gun, I would have waited. But I did leave a voicemail to tell you where I was going and why." I swore, lifting my right hand like I was going to swear over a bible or something. Not that anyone swearing over a book would keep them from lying—well, not without a *veritas* spell on said book.

"You left a voicemail." His accusing tone made my stomach bottom out, and I mentally crossed my fingers that the voicemail actually went through, and the cell phone gods weren't pissed at me, too.

Marcus narrowed his eyes as he took his phone from a pocket of his tactical pants, pressed a couple of buttons, put the phone to his ear, and listened. The scowl melted from his face, but the remaining expression was carefully blank. He was trying to keep me guessing, but I knew I had him. His eyebrows did that quiver thing that they did when he was trying to look stern, but really wanted to laugh.

Barrett, sensing the change in his husband, stepped around him to give me shit. "A four-hundred-year-old witch completely bypasses all her spells and mystical ways of contacting someone, and leaves a bloody voicemail. Humans have ruined you, Maxima."

I wanted to laugh at the joke, but all I could think was that they weren't the only ones. Ethereals had a hand in some of the worst of my ruin.

"You're probably right," I whispered, unable to laugh at the absurdity of it all, and Barrett's face fell a little. "Did you get an audience with the Fates?"

"Yes, but they either didn't have any information on the spikes or didn't want to share. I'm betting on the latter. Either way, we have nothing. You?"

"The whole courtroom was wiped. No evidence, not a speck of blood, nothing. I did a *revelare vestigium*, and it was brutal." I then launched into the tale of what we saw, stopping at the amulet. "I remembered Finn's, so we wanted to question him."

"We, huh?" Marcus huffed, staring at Alistair like he would rather crush him beneath his boot.

A sliver of hurt wound through me at that expression. Marcus had never looked at me like that, and I didn't know what Alistair had done to warrant it. Unable to stop myself, I stepped in between the two men—or further in between them.

"Yeah. He was there when I saw her. He helped me anchor the spell. We."

Marcus' eyebrows nearly reached his hairline, but he didn't comment any further on the "we" nonsense. "Very well, then. Finn, show us your amulet."

After hearing our every word, Finn was all too happy to help us. His only explanation was that he didn't want to get blamed for this shit. I had to give him that.

I studied the bronze disk Finn supplied—okay, he thrust it in my hand like it was on fire. The amulet was similar to the one I saw in the courtroom, but not the same. Finn's necklace was rough-hewn and ancient, the trident-like rune crudely carved into the metal. The amulet I saw in the courtroom was smoother, the three-pronged shape stamped instead of carved.

"This isn't like the one I saw, but it was similar. Like a trident, but without the recurve tines. Have any of you seen a necklace like that? On anyone?"

No one answered me until Finn piped up.

"Yeah. The witch I saw yesterday—the one who was supposed to undo your curse—"

"It's not a curse," Alistair and I said at the same time.

"Whatever," Finn shot back, exasperation written all over his face. "The witch. He had a necklace like that. I only noticed it because he tucked it away. He was going to help me, but then your Council found me and brought me back here. The guy split before he could even get started."

Barrett's face went white before color bloomed high on his cheeks. "What witch, Finn?"

Finn started to answer, then frowned, his mouth gaping like a fish as it opened and closed. Finn's face turned red, and I didn't understand until I caught the whiff of sea salt. I'd smelled that on the air last night but hadn't put it together.

Everything came crashing into place once Finn said the three words I dreaded most.

"I can't remember."

Memory spell.

Shit.

CHAPTER EIGHTEEN

Memory modification spells were the absolute worst. The last time I'd run across one, it had been done by a demon with limited to no finesse. More like a battering ram to the brain. The bartender's mind Micah had fricasseed ended up dead from me trying to pull the erased memories back. To this day, I still felt a heaving dose of guilt from my hand in Vaughn's death.

I could feel the horror cross my face at the thought of doing the same thing to Finn. I got it. Finn was a shit bag of the highest order. I still wasn't going to kill him unless I had to.

"Memory spell. The bad ones smell like rotten fish. This one is fresh—like salt water. I don't know what that means." My voice broke at my admission. I hated it when people messed with someone's mind. It was a violation.

"You can smell magic?" Alistair's tone was dubious.

I glanced over my shoulder at the idiot. "Of course I can. I see the threads of magic, too. Go ahead. Call me a freak. You wouldn't be the first."

I didn't have a lot of demon powers. I didn't phase into another shape like Alistair or Bernadette did. I didn't call to people like an incubus. What I didn't know about demons could fill a library, but I kind of hoped my weird extra-sensory shit was demon-based. The more disbelieving Alistair's face became, the less I reckoned that was likely. *Figures.*

I turned back to Barrett and Marcus who were looking at me like I'd lost my mind. "You guys knew this about me. Why is everyone staring at me like I'm a Martian or something?"

But the answer didn't come from my fellow Council members. It came from Alistair.

"Because that isn't a demon ability, nor is it a witch one." He said it like he knew what kind of power it was, and it wasn't good.

Honestly, I didn't want to know. If it was just another thing to knock me for a loop, I had exactly zero desire to pull that thread.

"Did you ever think that maybe since I'm the first of

my kind, maybe I have powers no one else does?" I shot back, trying to cover, but the hurt scalded my heart.

Of course I wasn't like anyone else. I did so relish being one of a kind. I enjoyed not looking like my mother or my father. I loved not sharing many features with my sister. I adored growing up with no family, moving every so often, losing friends, losing myself.

Honestly, it was my fucking favorite.

Alistair blinked at me, his plump lips mashed together like he hadn't thought of my oddness in just that way. Aces.

"Now that my freakishness is all out in the open, can we focus on the matter at hand? Someone messed with Finn's memory. I... don't trust myself to recover the ones he lost. The last time I tried, the man died."

Finn squawked like I'd shot him, and I didn't blame him. After I was done recovering what I could, Vaughn's brain was oozing out of his ears. Literally. I shook my head at Finn. Dickhead or not, I wasn't that cruel.

"Granted, the job done to his mind was cruder, and there wasn't much left to him, but... I don't want to. Are there other, less deadly ways to recover stolen memories? Or can we just hand him over to the Fates and tell them what we have?"

Barrett and Marcus seemed to think it over, but their posture was not optimistic.

Alistair, however, voiced his concerns right into my ear. "You killed a man?" His question made my head whip up to look at him square in the face.

My eyebrows shot up as I went for broke. "I've killed several. On purpose. Most of them grace your Hell as permanent residents. His death, however, was accidental. I'd never taken an innocent life before, and while he was a pawn in something bigger, he didn't deserve to die. Truth be told, I don't think he would have survived even without my intervention, but I carry the guilt all the same."

I spoke low and measured so he knew I was serious. Ninety-nine percent of the people I'd killed deserved it. Vaughn didn't, and that was why I didn't want to do a memory spell. My magic was wonky as hell right now, and I didn't trust it.

"I want to go to the Fates with this information. Unless they intervene, I don't know how we can move forward. Our only lead can't remember anything, which leaves us exactly fuck all to go on. And a memory spell that expertly crafted?" I paused, still meeting his gaze. "I could end up killing him and still get nothing."

"You don't like killing." Alistair said it like a complete and absolute truth like he was looking into my soul to measure my worth.

"Not innocent people, no. Not even a little."

"But bad people are okay?" He tilted his head a little, like he was trying to figure me out.

"Asks the Knight of Hell." I tilted my head in the same direction, taunting him. *Gotta stick to your strengths.*

I turned back to Marcus and Barrett who were still discussing what to do. "I'm going to the Fates with this. I love you both, but I'm not asking."

"I want to agree with you, but I know them, Max," Barrett began gently. "They are going to tell you this is nothing to go on. They'll say you brought them nothing but circumstantial evidence and your word, which to them, is nothing. Going to those three is a waste of time. Time we don't have."

I wanted to rip my hair out, but it was slicked back into a ponytail tight enough to make my scalp hurt. This whole thing was bullshit. "What would you have me do, huh? Unless you've got a better plan, I'm taking Finn, and we're going to the Fates."

I locked eyes with Finn. "I'm trying to keep you alive, okay? If I don't do this, either Barrett is going to do the reversal spell—which might kill you—or someone is going to come looking for the loose end. Either way, none of those options spell good things for you. So I'm taking you to them, and hopefully three damn deities have more magic than I do. But I swear on everything I love, if you fight me, I will snap your neck without a second thought, you got me?"

Finn showed me his teeth, which didn't spark much confidence. Then Finn's gaze slid to the man hovering just at my back—the same way he'd been doing it all damn day.

"And when you go to Hell—and you will go to Hell if you leave this earth today—I'll be the one making sure you stay there. Choose wisely, wolf. There won't be any more chances." Alistair's voice was a soft bit of cool menace wrapped in a blistering promise. He meant every single word.

And although he was threatening someone, I still felt that warmth threading through me that he gave a shit enough to back me up—even if he couldn't make his mind up about me.

"Fine. What the fuck am I going to do against the two of you, huh? This one"—He pointed to me—"made me no better than a human."

"As opposed to killing you in front of your entire pack like the coward you are. You tried to kick me when I was down, and then shifted and charged me in wolf form, you prick. Get your facts straight."

Alistair let out a quiet menace of a growl. It wasn't his angry animalistic one. No, this was something different. This was a sound pulled from nightmares.

This was the pit of Hell yawning wide and swallowing you whole.

"You are lucky I'm not your judge, wolf. But you'd better keep this in mind. When you go to Hell, there will be no place you can hide from me. Turn your life around before it's too late."

Marcus heaved a sigh before producing a key from his back pocket. "If he's going, I'm going to be there to make sure he doesn't lose his mind and try to escape. It's the least I can do for not watching him after he was sentenced."

"What else do I have to do today?" Barrett sighed. "Time to go get my ass handed to me again by a bunch of self-absorbed deities. Fun."

"Is it too much to ask that they come to us? We can't climb up Mount Olympus every time we need to check in," I griped, thinking of what kind of warding I'd need to put on Finn so he didn't do something stupid. Protection? Idiot-proofing?

THE TRIP TO AETHER WAS UNEVENTFUL. Mostly because it involved going upstairs and through one of the many doors that led to the underground witch club. The tricky part was not losing Finn once we got there. Even though Finn had human strength, speed, and abilities, I didn't put anything past him. I refused to get caught showing my ass because I was too lax on the wolf I'd spelled. Cursed.

Okay, it was probably a curse.

Bodies swarmed the dance floor as acrobats—or really skilled witches—swung and spun in the great swaths of fabric hanging from what seemed like nothing. They moved like they were underwater as lights flashed and danced over them. The sultry music had the patrons winding their bodies around one another.

The thing about Aether was, if you weren't a fan of nudity on an epic scale, this wasn't the place for you. It was almost as if the nakedness was to distract from all the doorways to other places. So far, it seemed like a solid protection. Who would notice the portals to other places with all the dicks hanging out?

Though, it also made me wonder if Dionysus was a witch, because this constant partying had to be supernatural.

We moved in a group through the throng, Barrett and Marcus in the front, Finn in the middle, and Alistair and I in the back, guarding our prisoner as we made our way to the right door. I felt uneasy, and I wanted it to be because I knew the Fates were going to be assholes. But something niggled at the back of my brain that Finn was a major loose end. And if the killer thought he was going to be able to lead back to him, he'd exterminate Finn without a second thought.

The crowd felt like it was closing in on us, like the swarm of bodies kept growing, multiplying until I almost couldn't breathe. A witch wearing nothing but a smile wrapped herself around Alistair, trying to get him to dance with her. Several people reached out and touched me, fingers tugged at my hair, pulled at my belt loops, stuck their fingers in my pockets. Hands reached for Finn, too, and that's when it became really fucking obvious something—or someone—might be behind this.

"Barrett!" I screamed when hands banded around me, yanking me off my feet and dragging me back into the swarm of bodies.

Then Marcus' training kicked in. I kicked up, throwing my legs up before swinging them back down, knocking my captor off balance before tossing him over the fulcrum of my hip.

But it wasn't just one. It was hundreds of people, some naked, some not. Some drunk or high or magicked out of their mind and all under a spell. Their faces blurred, swirled, as my breaths came in frightened pants. Their hands grabbed, held, and when my panic reached its crescendo, somehow my mind became sharp.

The ground quaked underneath our feet, the floor cracking and throwing people down as they tried to claw their way closer. Without a clear thought of why, I clapped my hands once, the concussion of that single motion knocking everyone within a twenty-foot radius on their asses. Acrobats slid from their ribbons, glass shattered, and still the earth quaked.

Barrett appeared in front of me, urging me to take deep breaths, to let the magic go. Pleading with me to stop because no one was attacking us anymore. But it was Alistair who managed to talk me down.

"Bloody hell, woman. You shake this building anymore, and the sodding roof will come down on us. You planning on killing us all?"

My panic throttled down, replaced with ultimate irritation. Granted, that made the earth stop quaking, but it wasn't like I was doing any of this on purpose.

"Don't tempt me, Knight," I growled through clenched teeth.

Barrett wrapped me in his arms, hugging me close for a beat longer than necessary. "You scared the shit out of us. But you saved us, too. So, thank you, Max, but can we never do that again?"

I let out a mirthless laugh as I pulled from Barrett's arms to look at the damage. Patrons lay on the floor in heaps. Unmoving.

"Did I kill them?" I murmured my question as tears flooded my eyes.

"No, Max. I put them under a sleeping spell. No telling how long it will last on some of them, so we need to go."

I nodded, surveying the sleeping bodies scattered like leaves on the dance floor. Someone had to know where we were going. Someone had to know we would bring Finn to the Fates. Someone had the time to spell all these people in a haven that was supposed to be safe.

"I hate to break it to you, Barrett, but you have one huge fucking leak."

CHAPTER NINETEEN

My gaze locked on Finn. He was cut up. So was Marcus, but Finn was hunched over, listing to the side like he'd been stabbed or was protecting an injured rib. Broken beer bottles and glass lay at his feet among the fallen bodies.

Human healing. Finn was going to die if I didn't do something.

"Finn?" I broke away from Barrett and Alistair.

He coughed once, red staining his lips as he staggered, and Marcus caught him. Scarlet blood leaked from the gaps in his fingers. Yep, he was definitely going to die if I didn't act.

Now.

"Yeah?" he muttered, his face going pale.

"If I give you back your wolf, will you get your shit

together and stop attacking people you think are weaker?"

He appeared confused, so I continued, "Meaning women, you fuck stick. No kicking people when they're down, no beating up on the little guy, no being a boil on the butt of humanity. Can you do that?"

An expression of hope crossed his face for a split second before he masked it. He gave me a weak nod.

"And get some anger management for shit's sake. It's the twenty-first century. Being a toxic douchebag is out. Think you can do that for me?"

Finn chuckled, his bitter laugh almost thready. "Yeah. If I make it through the day, I'll get right on that."

"Good. Don't make me regret this."

My hand knifed to Finn's chest, the pinky and thumb spread wide as I chanted the words for unlocking Finn's wolf, calling the other half of Finn's soul back to him.

Locking it up was easy. Letting it out? Not so much. Sweat popped up on my brow, my limbs turning to rubber as I called the white wolf back to his home. Using much more magic than it took to turn them off, I gave Finn everything I'd taken away. I gave him his healing, his wolf, his life.

I just hoped I wouldn't regret it.

"Now try not to die, mm-kay?"

I ripped my gaze off of Finn's rapidly healing wounds

when I caught someone's arm shifting a little out on the dance floor. "Barrett, lead the way. That spell is going to wear off, and soon."

The five of us shuffled off the dance floor, careful not to step on the unconscious but rousing bodies as we made our way to a corridor I'd never seen hidden behind a glamour. Everyone else saw a wall, but me? I saw the drafty hallway with no lighting and a cobblestone floor. Cobwebs fluttered in the corners of the entrance—either because no one noticed them, or because they added to the "get the fuck out of here" effect.

Barrett searched a bit on the wall, feeling for the break where the glamour met the real until I pointed out the opening.

"I always forget you can see through glamours. I swear it's like you have a Fae eye or something," he muttered, but I caught the words.

Fae eye?

"What the hell is a Fae eye?" I blurted, unable to hold in the question.

Barrett gaped at me like I was on drugs. "Some witch you are. Do you not read lore at all?"

I suppressed a shudder by the skin of my teeth. *Fairies.*

"Not about fucking fairies. They freak me out. All those rules, and they talk in riddles, and can't touch iron, and they trade for children's bones, and…" I did a full-body shudder. "Okay, so I watched *Pan's Labyrinth* one too many times and got freaked the fuck out. Sue me."

Barrett gave me a generous amount of side-eye. Whatever. That movie, along with every other one that had Fae shit in it was off the menu. Hard. Pass.

"Well, if you don't like trading for body parts, I'll keep my Fae-eye knowledge to myself," he quipped, leading the way through the pitch-dark corridor to the very last door.

I didn't even want to know.

He knocked three times and waited. Not a moment later, the arched door opened. It looked like the door to the witch's house in *Hansel and Gretel*.

Atropos stood in the doorway, not saying a word, barring our entry until I got fed up and walked up to her, not stopping until she obtained the good sense to move. The room was made of stacked stone, barren of everything that resembled comfort. No books, no chairs, not a single thing. Nothing but stone and more stone.

It was little better than a dungeon, and I'd seen enough of those to last a lifetime.

Atropos put her hands on her hips, irritated that I'd barged in. Whoops.

"What do you want? You can't be here to tell me *this* is the murderer."

So, I wasn't the only one she hated. Good to know.

"Atropos, meet Finn. Finn, this is Atropos, the cutter of the thread. She's super nice and loves all Ethereals."

She rolled her eyes at my blatant dig. "You're testing my patience, Maxima."

Testing her patience? Was she high? Sending me on a wild goose chase, and when I come to her all she can say is, I'm testing her patience?

"Awesome, you're irritating the fuck out of me, too. Glad we're even. Do you want to know why I dragged my entire friends list into your inner sanctum, or are you going to carry on being a complete jerk?"

She made the motion for me to carry on as she turned her back to us, seemingly leading the five of us down a spiral staircase. We followed, Finn in the middle of us all. I didn't begin speaking again until we reached the bottom.

This floor was much cozier than the last, the furnishings more cottage and less *Crime and Punishment*. Atropos took a seat on an overstuffed blood-red wingback chair, tossing her red braid over one shoulder so she could play with the strands.

"Finn here met with a witch yesterday after I cut him off from his wolf. He wanted this witch to reverse what

I'd done. Finn remembers the witch having an amulet like the one I saw in a *revelare vestigium* I performed on Ruby's death site. Trouble is, this witch modified Finn's memory. I can't move forward with the investigation without knowing who the witch is, and I have a moral quandary with noodling with someone's noodle."

Lachesis crossed her feet on her midnight-blue ottoman which matched her wingback. "You say you cut him off from his wolf, but he has the animal roiling under his skin. You forgive him so soon?"

Lachesis could see Finn's wolf, then. Interesting.

"He was dying. He promised to behave, so I gave it back. If he doesn't hold up his end of the bargain, I'll kill him."

"For a little game of chicken? Surely, you're overreacting." Atropos sneered, downplaying what he did.

"No, I'm not overreacting," I said calmly, trying not to let this certified bitch get a rise out of me. "And I don't appreciate you saying so. Had I not done what I did, Marcus would have had to kill him. I know you thirst for death, but I don't. Now, are you going to help us figure this shit out, or what?"

Atropos' face was snide like she was going to throw in another dig. But I stopped her before she started.

"Look, the entirety of Aether just attacked us so we wouldn't get to you. They were spelled, heavily. So, whoever did it has more mojo than I've seen in a while. I have a feeling this witch doesn't want us coming to you with this, which makes me want to come to you. You can put us on the right path, so please, just do me a solid and quit your bullshit. I don't know what the fuck I did to you to piss you off, but honestly, I'm doing my best here."

"There is nothing we can do to recover the memory without killing him, but you knew that already. That is why you won't do it yourself," Lachesis said, not unkindly.

"Well, I thought you had more power than I did." I blew out a breath, throwing up my hands.

All three of them looked at me like I was a Martian, like I'd said something so absurd they couldn't believe my stupidity. Fair enough.

Clotho—who had been silent up to now, comfortable to let her sisters do the talking—asked a very important question. "What did the amulet look like? The one that was on the neck of the murderer."

I closed my eyes to make sure I described it right. "It was like a trident, but not. Three-pronged. The left and right angled inward, and the middle straight, but with no recurve on the tines and a single line under the trident. It had Latin stamped around the edges, too. *Cineres cineribus pulverem pulveri.*"

Ashes to ashes, dust to dust. I'd forgotten that detail until just now.

"I've never seen anything like it, I don't think. Have any of you?"

Silence reigned for a long moment.

Atropos sat up in her chair from her formerly relaxed position. "We cannot help you, and all you're doing is wasting our time. You performed a *revelare vestigium* which cannot be replicated. Who else saw this amulet besides the unreliable werewolf witness?"

"Me. I saw everything Max did," Alistair said from behind me. "She speaks the truth."

"And what is the word of a Quinn worth?" Clotho was not snide, not teasing. Like she really wanted to know how much stock he placed in his word.

"My family is not me." He stepped in front of me, and just for a moment, glancing over his shoulder like he was studying my face, reluctance on his. "And my word is worth quite a bit. It is worth blood and war, worth life and death."

Alistair sounded like he was making a promise to Clotho, but I didn't understand what kind of commitment he was swearing to.

"Be that as it may, we can't go on the testimony of a faulty mind, and we can't see the *revelare vestigium* for ourselves," Lachesis began.

Shit. Why did I do that damn spell?

Atropos picked up where she left off. "And our order stands. Bring the killer to us. You have thirty-six hours to complete your task. No exceptions."

Atropos and Lachesis stood, leaving the five of us with Clotho. She seemed reluctant to rise and follow her sisters, a frown marring her young face.

"This does not make sense. You don't make any sense." She seemed to mutter to herself before looking up at me specifically from her perch on her bubble-gum-pink chair. "You should know the symbol you described, but you do not. You should know your own power after these many centuries, but you do not. You should know these things, but you claim otherwise. I do not know if you are dishonest, or if you are just in the dark." She said these words in a whisper as if she didn't want her sisters to hear.

"I cannot help you find what you need, but you have someone close to you who can." She paused as if she was checking to see if her sisters were out of earshot before she began again. "Ask Teresa about the amulet you described. She will tell you everything you need to know." Clotho peered over her shoulder to the hallway her sisters had walked down. "I suggest you do not come back until you have found what was asked of you. Atropos and Lachesis do not do well with souls on their journey. We were never meant to interfere, and when we do, there is always a cost."

A cost? Atropos and Lachesis interfered in Ethereal business by putting me in charge of this, and now it was costing them. They put me in charge of this. Because they thought I could do it? Or as punishment for some slight I had no idea I was making? And every time someone came to them, it took a toll. I didn't know what I thought about that—or the fact that Teresa somehow knew about the amulet we had been searching for.

None of this set well with me.

"Thank you for the guidance, Clotho. I appreciate it."

The blonde Fate smiled at me—a sad, lonely little smile.

That wane upturn to her lips made me wonder if it had cost her, too.

CHAPTER TWENTY

Kicking up little puffs of dust with every step, I reluctantly inched toward my mother's farmhouse on the outskirts of Coeur 'd Alene. The last time I made this trek, I had a demon brand on my arm and a knife to procure. The demon was dead now, and so was the blade, and since that day, my relationship with my mother had taken a very different turn. Still, old habits died hard, and if I didn't have people with me, I likely wouldn't be here in the first place.

"If you move any bloody slower, you'd be going backwards. We're on the clock, you know."

Alistair's crisp British accent was like a knife in my brain, but I didn't say anything. I wouldn't give him the satisfaction of seeing me scared of my mommy.

But this wasn't a social visit, and I didn't actually have the time to be this reluctant, so I gave him a dirty look over my shoulder and picked up the pace. Marcus and Barrett were busy dropping Finn off in his new home of the dungeon—just until we could figure out what to do with him—so I picked up my vampire assistant, and the three of us—Della, Alistair, and I—made the journey the quick way.

Through another door. Sometime—when the Apocalypse wasn't upon us—I would have to talk to Barrett about those damn doors.

Unlike the last time, there was no bevy of guards between me and the porch. There was no one. The absolute lack of people protecting my mother did not sit well with me. It wasn't so long ago that there had been an attack on all the major coven leaders. Only two managed to survive, Teresa among them.

She was waiting for me on the porch—not in her bathrobe, at least—her foot tapping impatiently on the wood planks.

"You could have called, Maxima. I would have come to you."

This was a much better reception than the last time I was here, which immediately made me think she was up to something. Taking in her casual attire and almost happy expression, I figured I knew exactly why there were no guards here.

Automatically, my eyes narrowed. "My father is here, isn't he?"

Andras was my mom's first love, so the fact that they reconnected kind of made sense if you didn't look too hard at the last four hundred years of abandonment and general fuckery.

"He was, but I don't know why that would bother you." Her voice had that dreamy quality of a woman full up on orgasms, and I kinda wanted to deck her.

I had several reasons to be bothered, one of which was my parents getting back together. The last thing the universe needed was another one of me walking around. Plus, the last time they got all loved up, they completely forgot to look for my little sister, Maria. Stellar parenting right there. Honestly, I didn't have time to deal with my parents' relationship issues.

"It doesn't matter. Have bigger problems than what you two decide to do to one another." And there would be bloodshed and tears if history was anything to go by. "An angel is dead, Mother, I kinda need your help."

She invited us in, pouring me a cup of coffee, but mostly ignoring Della and flat-out refusing to look at Alistair.

I filled Teresa in on the gory details of Ruby's

murder, along with the even further concerning task the Fates decided to fuck me over with. But the more I talked, the quieter my mother became until she stopped talking altogether.

This didn't feel right.

Especially since Andras knew all about the murder, and Mom was pretending like she was just now hearing of it. That, and when I took a sheet of paper and drew the amulet for her, she went gray.

"Mom. Clotho pretty much told me to ask you what this meant, so you're going to spill."

But still, she said nothing.

I got up from my stool and grabbed Teresa's shoulders, shaking the shit out of her, because honestly? I did not have the time or energy to get into a battle of wills with my mother.

But her head just rocked on her neck, and still, she didn't talk, didn't react. That's when I noticed the dark magic roiling in her hair. I would like to think I didn't notice because the magic was masked in the darkness of her hair, but it was more likely that I just didn't bother to look.

"What's wrong with her?" Della's voice was no more than a whisper, just in case my mother could hear us.

"Dark magic is swirling around her head, so I'm going with someone doesn't want her to talk."

I wanted to believe my father wasn't capable of something like this, but the black, smoky motes practically screamed Andras.

"I'm going to help you, Mom," I murmured. "Don't you worry."

Concentrating on the motes of power, I saw them like a snarl of knots in my mind. One by one, I worked to untangle them from her. Freeing her bit by bit, I only got angrier. Andras did a number on my mother, and I wanted to know why.

When the last knot was undone, Teresa sucked in a big breath like she had been held underwater, and then it was no longer me holding her up, but the other way around.

"What in the Fates? Max? What is everyone doing in my kitchen?"

Alistair gave the simplest of conclusions. "Your ex is a right bastard, that's what."

Teresa whipped her head in his direction, her eyes narrowing at the accusation until her brain caught up. Her face went slack for a split second before rage colored her very being. "I swear to the Fates, when I'm done with that man, he'll wish I could kill him."

I slumped into a chair at the breakfast nook table. "Good, you're on board. Now did Andras tell you what is going on? About Ruby?"

"The angel that was murdered? Yes, but he…" She trailed off. "I'm sorry, I can't remember much of what he said. Something about how the Fates were going to blame a demon…"

I nodded, wishing my coffee was in arm's reach. "You're looking at her. I have about thirty-five hours left to find the bastard, and I need your help. I'm assuming Andras spelled you so he could look for the culprit on his own?"

"That sounds like something he would do." Teresa rubbed a hand over her face like she couldn't believe her ex could be that stupid, even though we both knew that this was a case of history repeating itself.

"So, you're telling me your father would rather cut you out of finding the man who tried to frame you, rather than let either of you two help?" Della's husky accent curled her words in complete disbelief.

"It wouldn't be the first time," I answered her.

"I've been in your presence less than a day, and I already know better than that. He knows you even less than I do." Alistair's words weren't meant to be barbed, but they still stung.

"Mom, do you know anything about this symbol?" I showed her the drawing I'd sketched.

Her face went gray again, and I felt it on the air when she lied. "No. It doesn't look familiar."

I nodded and caught Della's gaze. We'd planned for this, my mother being tight-lipped. And while I had reservations about messing with her mind, I did not have any whatsoever about Della doing it.

Della stood up, holding her hand out for my mother to shake. "Teresa, we've never met, I'm Della."

As soon as Della's fingers closed around my mother's, she yanked her closer, making sure she snagged her gaze. As soon as Teresa's eyes locked on Della's, Della started to speak in a haunting, almost hypnotic way.

"We are not going to hurt you, so you aren't going to be afraid. You will answer our questions honestly and without hesitation. You will not hide things from us. Do you understand?"

"Yes, I understand." Teresa's voice was monotone and dead. The sound made me shudder.

"Mom, do you know anything about this symbol?" I repeated, holding up the sketch.

Teresa nodded. "It is an Arcadios amulet—a necromancy symbol and motto. But it did more than that. It held the power of a harnessed demon. Only our elders had them."

No wonder she didn't want to say.

"Do you have one?"

Teresa shook her head. "I salted the bronze and burned it in a forging fire when I decided to turn the coven in the week before you were shunned. I watched it melt, felt the power return to the demon I was bound to."

I narrowed my eyes, studying my mother anew. My mother used to be a necromancer. She turned in her coven for a wrongdoing of some sort. My mother was bound to a demon, and I had a sneaking suspicion, my father was the one she was bound to. Maybe she still was.

"Does anyone else have one that you know of? Maybe one of the other elders?"

"All of the other elders were executed. You, Maria, and I are the only Arcadios members left."

That was news to me. What the fuck had they done to get a whole coven wiped out?

"Why was the coven…" I trailed off, trying to think of the appropriate word. "Disbanded? And why would you turn them in? Turn them in for what?"

"Necromancy wasn't always outlawed. It used to be frowned upon, but never against the law. Our coven was the reason it was. Our coven didn't just steal a demon's power. They made deals—deals they never should have made. They promised bodies of our children to inhabit demons who didn't have a corporal form. In exchange, the demon would bring another to tether—to drain. The first time it was done, no one cared because the child had recently died. Then we learned the child was a sacrifice, and no one seemed to care but me. Drunk on power, they were offering up their children to slaughter. The night you were burned? They wanted you or Maria to be an offering, but I couldn't watch you both, and I couldn't free you both if you were chosen, so I only brought her."

There was more to the story, but I didn't have to wait for Teresa to continue.

"Everyone knew you were different. There was no way I could bring you. If the demon chose you, everyone would know what you were, because you wouldn't die. So, I brought Maria. Luckily, she wasn't chosen, so I didn't blow my cover, but another child was sacrificed. As I called the Keys, you dropped the ward. While you were burning, nearly every member of our coven, except for Maria and I, were carted off to the Council. The demon we were trying to put into the child's body was dragged back to Hell, and you were shunned so no one would know about what you were. I was afraid either your family would come looking for you, or the Keys would mistake you for a possessed child. As far as I know, no coven member survived."

"Well, someone passed one down or found one, because our killer had an amulet just like that." I pointed to the drawing. "They had to have missed someone. They missed me, it's entirely possible."

"What about the other children? Did they kill them, too?" Della's voice was horrified.

Teresa looked at her and nodded. "Yes. All of them. They burned our encampment to the ground. Nothing was left."

But that wasn't true. I had an athame from the refuse of that encampment. And who knew what Maria had taken with her as a child. Something could have survived. And as much as it worried me, someone could have survived as well.

I didn't trust that the Keys—not that I'd been in the presence of these Ethereals for more than the five minutes it took to cart me to a cell—killed every man, woman, and child.

Someone survived. Someone had an amulet, and he knew how to use it. And he didn't just kill Ruby. He drained her power and was using it.

I needed to call Maria again. If someone was targeting me and mine, it was entirely plausible they would target her, too.

Whipping out my phone, I had her contact up and was listening to her phone ring and ring. Why the fuck wasn't she answering?

"Della, have you heard from Maria? I haven't been

able to get ahold of her and I want to make sure she's safe."

"No, I haven't talked to her."

For some reason, Della didn't look at me. She didn't even turn around. And while I felt the truth in her words, she was still hiding something from me.

My stomach dropped, dread seeping into every fiber of what made me who I was. Something was wrong. Someone was lying. And Della knew something.

Where the fuck was my sister?

CHAPTER TWENTY-ONE

I didn't notice the ground shaking until Alistair put a hand on my shoulder, and even then, the shudders that shook the house and everything in it didn't stop. I just knew about them now.

Magic bloomed hot over my fingers, twirling and writhing like snakes along my flesh and nearly as solid. The panes of glass in my mother's cabinets splintered and cracked, the sound of them shattering only adding to the disquiet that coalesced into a shroud of rage permeating every fiber of my body.

Something was wrong with my sister, and Della knew. She knew and didn't tell me.

"Della, where is my sister? And where is Striker? Moreover, what in my past behavior led you to believe lying to me was a good idea? Answer in any order you choose." My voice sounded calm, which wasn't a good sign. Calm with this much rage meant that killing people wasn't off the menu.

A part of me knew that I was probably overreacting. The other part of me gave the rational side the finger and went on displaying her fury.

"I didn't lie. I haven't spoken to her since the presentation." Della dodged my questions, still unable to meet my eyes.

The house shuddered again and plates fell from the cabinets, shattering on the stone floor. Wind whipped inside the kitchen, tossing all our hair into snarled knots, but I didn't care. I wanted answers.

"You still know where she is, though. And wherever that is, isn't safe. Where is my sister, Della?"

"I promised I wouldn't tell. I swore that I wouldn't distract you."

The ground shifted once again and then stilled.

"Promised who?" I asked, but I already knew.

Della bit her lips, shifting on her feet as she reached into the back pocket of her jeans. I'd never seen her so dressed down. It should have been a dead giveaway that she was in the middle of some shit.

"I promised Striker. I swore that I wouldn't let you divert yourself because you didn't have the time to look for Maria and the killer. But we didn't know. Not until we got this..." She trailed off, handing me a folded paper.

The rich lettering was on heavy cardstock, rough, like it purposely didn't have a finished edge. On the outside in a beautiful script, it simply said "For Maxima" in a scrawl I'd only seen once. Only the last time I saw it, the ink was blood.

I flipped open the card.

I gave you a gift.
Now, it's time to return the favor.

My mind blanked for a single hot second, and then the ground pitched, knocking everyone but me off their feet. The stone counter cracked, sliding off the cabinet below and shattering on the floor. And still, I didn't stop. Walls split, fissures erupted in the floor, Alistair and Della yelled for me. And still, I didn't stop.

I wanted to do what I had with Alistair. I wanted to summon Striker into a circle and then beat him to death with his own severed limbs. And because I knew he wouldn't be alone—let's face it, lately Striker was never without Aidan or Ian—I wanted them in their own circles just so I could smack them upside their heads.

"Maxima, none of this is helping your sister. You need to stop now." Teresa's arms encircled me from the side as she whispered soothing words in my ear. In all my life, I couldn't remember my mother hugging me. Not ever. Not even as a small child with a cut knee. But she did then, murmuring lies in my ear to calm me down.

That we would find her. That we would bring Maria home safe. That we could fix this.

But could we?

Could we fix anything? Or would we only make it worse?

The ground stilled again, and the house groaned once, and then settled. I met Della's fearful expression with one of my own. I had to give her credit. Even with me close to losing my control, she still kept her fangs put away.

"Take me to Striker," I ordered, and she complied.

THE FIRST THING I DID ONCE I SAW STRIKER and Aidan poring over Arcadios lore books, was snap my fingers and watch gleefully as their heads knocked together like a *Three Stooges* skit. After that, I looked around the open-concept flat that took up the entire bottom floor of what used to be a warehouse. Striker's new abode.

Everything was high end. The mahogany table that

could seat twenty. The Persian rug that had to be over twenty grand all on its own. The giant tricked-out kitchen with custom concrete counters. Modern yet traditional with the price tag to match. He always did have expensive taste.

Aidan gave me a dirty look as he rubbed his temple. But Striker was the one with some sense, because he took a few steps back and raised his hands in an attempt to placate me.

"Max—"

"Why would you cut me out of this?" I growled. "It's Maria, Striker. You know better."

"It wasn't like that. We had no idea—"

"What? That the cretin who killed Ruby was the same man who took my sister? Weird? It's like I could have given you that information if you'd have fucking asked me."

Betrayal like I'd never felt before stole through me. This wasn't the first time he'd done this— left me out of the loop. He'd done it with Melody, too, using me and my power to get revenge. He'd gone behind my back and done things because he thought he'd known better. It seemed they all did that.

Aidan stepped in between us and tried to come to Striker's defense. "It wasn't his idea to leave you out. We all saw what you were like when Andras took your mother. We thought you'd lose it and abandon your investigation."

"Oh, so it's your fault one of my best friends seems to have forgotten a century's worth of time with me to follow your lead. Good to know," I said sarcastically as I flicked my fingers at Aidan and watched him fly back, smack the closest wall, and crumple into a heap on the ground.

The said ground shook again, only this time fire sprung up with it, lighting all the candles that stood tall in candelabras and chandeliers. Thunder rumbled loud enough to be heard over the din of the earth shaking. The crack of lightning nearly split the whole world in two.

I drew the athame from the sheath concealed in my belt, pressing the rune just under the first curve in the hilt so the blade expanded into a short sword. The green of my magic raced down the metal to coat the edge in liquid green fire.

"As many times as you've betrayed me, I always took you back, always kept you with me, because I thought you did it out of love. But this… this is something else. This is you not trusting me to know something vital. This is you proving that you don't care about me."

I took a step toward Striker, lightning cracking outside as my heel hit the floor.

"No, Max. I know how much you love your sister. I know you would do anything for her. I didn't want you to put her first."

Selfish.

"You thought I would risk everything, drop everything, and what? Let the world burn?" I seethed through gritted teeth. "You don't know me at all. A century of you being my friend, and you know nothing."

A lightning strike hit once, twice, three times, the rumble of the thunder almost instant. The power went out in Striker's flat, as the candles' flames rose higher and higher. A line of fire raced for Striker before splitting to encircle him, caging him inside the flames.

"As many times as you have betrayed me, I should kill you," I whispered. "I ought to just snuff you out."

How many times had he done this to me? Ten? A hundred? Thought he knew better, and I was the one left on the outside?

"This isn't a betrayal. This is me protecting you, can't you see that? It's what I've done a hundred times, a thousand. It is what I've always done."

"Yes, it's what you've always done. And I'm not going to take it anymore. I'm not some idiot without a brain in her head, Striker. I'm a grown woman with centuries of life and death under my belt. It's not me who is in the wrong here. It's you."

The earth shuddered again, creating cracks and fissures in the floor. Some so deep, the heat of the earth seeped up ready to swallow us all. Then I felt a different heat at my back, and before I knew it, I had arms around me—one banding over my chest, the other around my waist. Not pulling, not containing, just holding.

"Love, I'm going to have to ask that you not kill the angel if at all possible. I'd hate to prevent a war by starting it, if you catch my meaning."

Alistair's words were soft, peaceful in the face of my destruction. I'd almost forgotten he was here.

"This isn't finding your sister, Max. Ramp down your magic, and then we can start looking. Together."

I didn't want to ramp down my magic. I didn't want my fire snuffed out and shoved back in the box at the back of my brain. I didn't want to stop being angry. I wanted them to know that I wasn't going to take this shit anymore.

I wasn't going to be left out and left behind. I wasn't going to be the one no one wanted to confide in or trust with their secrets.

I wasn't.

"Let him go, love. He didn't mean to disrespect you. He didn't know it would hurt you so. He isn't your enemy, Max."

Alistair was right. Striker wasn't my enemy—it didn't

mean he was my friend, either. But Striker never hurt me on purpose. He was just an idiot with a god complex.

So, I closed my eyes and mentally shoved all my unleashed power back into the little box that held it. I let the ground stop churning, let the storm clouds go so they could dissipate into vapor. And I let the fire die. In my mind, I sealed all the cracks and fissures, put them back the way they were before I lost my temper.

"That's good, love. Very good. Now, all you have to do is put that blade away, and you'll be all done."

I turned my head so I could look Alistair in the eye. "I don't want to."

"Yes, I understand that, but you're scaring the bollocks off everyone in the room, and I think you're going to have to, love. Common courtesy and all that rot."

Grumbling, I unseeingly found the rune and pressed it, letting the blade collapse in on itself, and then sheathed it.

Alistair gave me a soft smile like I'd pleased him in some way. "I'm sure I'll never forget this, but, remind me never to underestimate you."

I wanted to tell him that if the summoning incident didn't teach him that, then nothing would, but I managed to hold my tongue. Especially since Ian and

Andras picked that exact moment to walk through a portal door in the west wall.

As soon as my mother saw Andras, she snapped her fingers and set his head on fire, which made him drop the bags of takeout he and Ian apparently left to procure. I held in a snort by the skin of my teeth, and my father gave my mother a scathing glare. The fire wouldn't hurt him, but it was hilarious to watch.

"What the hell was that for?" Andras grumbled as he batted out the flames.

I braced for my mother to lose her mind like I did, but she didn't. Instead, she ignored my father and held her hand out for the card that Della had given me.

"Give me that card, and let's find your sister before I figure out how to really hurt him."

I passed the card to her, but the message she saw wasn't the only one written there. It was just the only one she could see. As soon as my fingers touched the parchment the first time, another message began writing itself underneath the first. The magic in the swirling letters somehow telling me I would be the only one to know what it said.

But the message was clear enough.

Come to me. Come alone. Let's make a trade.

Me for Maria.

Hadn't that always been the way?

There wasn't a doubt in my mind that I'd come to him, but I didn't think he'd like what happened when I got there.

I was getting my sister back. The question was if I would get him to the Fates or kill him and fuck everyone else over.

Only one way to find out.

CHAPTER TWENTY-TWO

Watching the clock was my new pastime. While the rest of them argued about the right thing to do, I sat on a barstool and ate my way through a carton of orange chicken, watching said clock tick away. If I was going out—and I had a feeling I was—then I wanted the yummy goodness of fake Chinese food in my belly before I went. Then I was going to lie my ass off and go get my sister.

And hopefully, stop the lunatic who wanted to jump-start the apocalypse. And why was that always the goal? Evil super villains always wanted either the end of the world, or power and the end of the world. Honestly, what had power ever done for anyone except paint a massive target on their backs?

Aidan and Ian were whispering off in a corner, Della

was refereeing my parents, Striker was pouting and trying to catch my eye—probably so he could apologize—and Alistair was perched next to me, trying to swipe the last cream cheese wonton.

Not on my watch, pal.

Like the lady I was, I slapped the fried goodness out of his hand and stuffed it whole into my mouth, much to Alistair's chagrin.

"You are all class, Maxima. Anyone ever tell you that?"

Was that a pout on his face? Surely not.

"Nope," I replied, but it sounded more like "noupf."

Alistair turned me on my barstool, fitting my legs between his. Surprised, I kept right on munching, but the man had my attention.

"The others might not get what you're about to do, but I know you're planning something. I trust you know what you're doing, but I want in—whatever it is." His voice was low and soft, almost a whisper.

I shook my head, but he put a hand over mine to further get my attention. I gave it.

"I saw your face, love. I've known you long enough to know when you're planning something."

I snorted—*totally ladylike, I swear*—and nearly busted out laughing. "You've known me for less than a day."

His lips twisted in an arrogant half-smile. "I pay attention."

I debated on what I should say—if anything at all. So far, Alistair was the only person in this room to not make me feel like shit. But I still didn't quite trust him. His earlier words filtered through my brain.

How exactly is a man supposed to earn your trust if you refuse to give him even an ounce of leeway to prove himself?

But this was a hell of a lot of leeway.

Sighing, I gave in. "He wants me. He'll trade for Maria."

"And you're thinking of going." Not a question. See? The guy really did know me.

I nodded before stuffing another piece of tart chicken in my mouth. "I don't know if he'll really give her up, but I don't gamble with Maria's life. I never have."

"You don't want them to know." Another not-question.

I thought of all the times I'd tried to make a plan, only to have it blow up in my face because of either Striker, my father, or my mother. Yeah… no. I shook my head. "The quickest way to see my plan go to shit is to tell one of these tools. I'd rather just do it myself and save the hassle." *Said every other Virgo ad nauseam until the end of fucking time.*

"Need any backup? I'm great at following directions."

He gave me a wolfish grin that made one of his dimples pop.

Fates, was his smile made of napalm or something? I had the inexplicable urge to fan myself.

"I was told to come alone. I fully expect you to follow me though, so try not to get yourself killed. I'll feel really bad about it later." I was trusting him on this, because if he didn't follow, there was a distinct possibility I would get remarkably screwed.

"I can feel your concern, really," Alistair deadpanned, his sarcasm so thick you could cut it.

The truth of it was, I would feel horrible if he got hurt, the same as I would if any of them got hurt for me. Didn't Striker understand that? Did any of them?

But this wasn't about me. This was about Maria.

"You need a distraction? That why you've been staring at the clock like you're trying to set it on fire with your mind?"

Way. Too. Perceptive.

"Pretty much. I need a way to slip out of here with enough lag time so no one follows me for a bit. I have a feeling he'd know." By he, I meant the killer, but I had a feeling Alistair knew.

"I've got an idea on that, but you might not like it. Really, though, I have put in quite a lot of time considering the best way to get you out of here with no one following you, and this, by far, is the best way I can think of." He took the carton of chicken out of my hands, setting it on the counter.

His expression was earnest enough that I was willing to entertain hearing him out, but skepticism was my BFF and true love all wrapped up in one. Resting my chin on my hand, I leaned conspiratorially closer, waiting for this master plan he spoke of. "Go on."

Instead of answering me, Alistair moved closer—and I didn't think we could get much closer than we already were—his breath hitting my lips as he whispered a warning, "Don't freeze."

I didn't understand until his lips lowered, hitting mine in the most delicate of clashes.

"Kissing me is your master plan?" Our mouths were so close, my lips brushed his as I spoke.

"Not exactly," he murmured before his fingers cupped my chin, and his mouth landed on mine.

No brushes. No teasing. Just his pillowy soft, yet oh-so-firm lips on mine. My hands somehow found themselves hooked on his nearly scalding biceps, heat radiating through every bit of him. I couldn't tell if that was my imagination or not, and once his tongue touched my bottom lip, I really didn't give a shit. Then I was up and off the barstool, with my legs wrapped around Alistair's waist, and at no point did our mouths not touch. We were moving, I was sure, but all I felt was his heat filtering through me and his hands on my ass as he carried me to wherever we were going.

Hopefully, it was somewhere with a bed.

In the back of my mind, I heard the soft snick of a latch closing, but again, I was busy making out with the hot-as-sin Knight of Hell. When was the last time I made out with anyone? It felt like it had been ages.

The heat of Alistair's hands—hell, his whole body—radiated through me on a visceral level, causing shudders of want to roll over me. My back met cool metal as Alistair pressed closer, the bulge in his jeans pressing on just the right spot. I moaned into his mouth as my arms wound around his neck. My fingers found their way to his hair, gripping the curls so I could get closer.

Alistair groaned, pressed himself against me once more, and then broke the kiss, the pair of us sucking in huge breaths of air as we stared hungrily at each other.

"I'm pretty sure no one is going to follow us after that. And while I would really love to see if you have tattoos in places I haven't seen, I'm going to be a gentleman and put you down."

The distraction. Right. I'd somehow forgotten that was his master plan. Disappointment crashed into me until I realized Alistair hadn't yet put me down and was still staring at my face.

"What?"

"This isn't me leaving you behind. This is me trying to do the right thing with only a slight benefit to myself."

His sly grin had me tightening my legs around his waist so the in-no-way-slight bulge in his jeans rubbed against me once again.

"I don't think slight is in your vocabulary." I unwrapped my legs from his hips, and he let me down. And by let me down, I mean he ever so slowly let my body slide down his, the heat of him wringing just one more shudder out of me. And even though he let me down, he didn't let me go.

His hands made themselves at home at the curve of my hip as he wound his fingers around my belt loops. "I'd say you have about a fifteen-minute head start. I wish it could be more, but with this lot, that is about as much privacy as they'll manage. How do we find you?"

I thought about it for a second before pulling one of the amulets off my neck and fastening it around Alistair's, it's twin still resting against my chest. I grasped the obsidian ovals, whispering the words I needed so he could find me wherever I was if I wore its twin.

"You'll find me just fine, I think."

I took a step back, but Alistair refused to let me go. "I want you to watch out for yourself while you're saving your sister. Take only the risks you need to take. As much as you say different, there are people out there who care about you, who want you, who need you. When you're thinking there is no one, you're wrong. I want you to remember that. Remember that I'm coming for you. Do you understand?"

I swallowed thickly as I nodded, trying to hold back the wetness that hit my eyes. "I'll remember."

Only then did Alistair let me go.

I pointed my feet east toward the beacon that had sounded in my brain once I decided to meet with the man who'd taken my sister. Who killed Ruby. Who in all likelihood, wanted to kill me.

I let myself glance back once and met Alistair's somber gaze with one of my own. I mouthed the words "I'll remember" at him, but that only earned me a slight tip to his lips.

Only then did I snap my fingers, taking me away from him and toward the darkness.

CHAPTER TWENTY-THREE

When my feet touched down on forest bracken, I knew without a doubt I'd already fucked up. I'd tried to adjust course, tried to arrive a few miles away so I could walk in undetected. No dice. Somehow, the spell he used on the parchment—which seemed coded to me specifically—hijacked my landing. Somehow, some way, he must have gotten ahold of my blood? That was the only way I knew how to tune a spell for just one person.

Trees surrounded me except for a small clearing, the moonlight barely filtering through them, but I didn't have to worry about the darkness. No, darkness wasn't an issue at all due to the lit torches dotting the landscape in regular intervals. It lit the center of the clearing perfectly.

The center of the clearing that had a stone altar. With my sister on it.

The altar was little more than a giant quartz boulder flattened either by man or by time—either way, it made a pretty clear picture of what was at stake. Maria was no longer in her pretty presentation day dress. Instead, she seemed to be dressed in some kind of old-timey nightgown with a high collar held together by threaded ties. I used to have one like it as a teen, the coarse linen always seeming to chafe my neck, and I was glad when modern sleepwear shifted from those puritan trappings.

I felt eyes on me even though it wasn't Maria. No, Maria was too busy looking at the back of her own eyelids, the motes of what appeared to be a sleep spell glittered and popped near her face. Sleeping would definitely be better than worrying about her potential for sacrifice. Which seemed high.

And even though I knew eyes were on me, I still had to try and get Maria the hell out of here. But every step seemed too loud, like the snapping twigs would summon someone here to stop me. I stepped more carefully, slowly making my way to Maria, but when I felt a shiver of magic race across my skin, I quit the careful bullshit and raced to her. Ten feet from the boulder that held my sister, I hit a wall of magic, tossing me off my feet.

My body airborne, it felt like lightning ricocheted across my skin. It burned and twisted, like when I'd gotten backlash with Alistair's summoning circle, only twice as bad. I hit the ground and skidded, the twigs and mulched undergrowth ripping at my skin, tearing at it like they had fingers with knives for nails.

"*Tsk, tsk, tsk*. I thought you'd know better, Maxima," a familiar voice called, but I couldn't place it. A young-ish man walked out from the cover of the trees. Or at least he looked young from twenty feet away and through the hazy lenses of the recently electrocuted.

"Knowing better isn't really my specialty." I said this from my hands and knees before I retched in the dirt—a testament to my statement if there ever was one. There went the orange chicken. One of these days I was going to be able to keep the food I ate in my stomach.

"That seems clear. You don't appear to pay attention, now do you? It took a hell of a lot of effort to get your attention, Maxima, and even then, it took you far too long to realize your sister had even been taken."

"I have stubborn friends and a very unhelpful batch of allies." I shrugged as best I could while still having a death grip on my stomach. "That doesn't always lend to timeliness. You wanted my attention. Now you have it."

The man came closer, and I studied him as best as I could while still hoping my stomach didn't decide to worm its way up my throat. He was slender, but not emaciated. Just small. No taller than I was, maybe five eight at a push. Dressed in a dove-gray three-piece suit, he seemed almost dapper, like he would be going to a business meeting after this.

Ritual sacrifice at seven, business meeting at eight.

He had medium-brown hair that hung to his shoulders and a heavy brow that made his face almost kind if it weren't for the crazy light in his eyes. Those were the eyes of a man that did not give a single fuck and wanted you to know it.

Yep. This was a horrible plan. Whose idea was it for me to go in alone? *Oh, yeah. Mine.*

"But do I? Do you know all the things I did to get you to notice? All the favors I racked up? You didn't notice when your old flame Enzo dropped off the map, now did you? He disrespected you so much when he left you, didn't he? But I didn't let that stand."

Enzo? It had been decades since I'd heard that name. Lorenzo Costa dated me for a very short summer in the 1920s. Everything had been fine until he'd found out I was a witch—or rather, when he'd found out I was a Rogue. I never saw him again after the day he learned who I was, but at the time, I didn't blame him. Our entire relationship had been one big lie. It was doomed to end as soon as it had begun, and I didn't blame him. Not one bit.

"You never heard from those incubi again, did you? Micah Goode had friends, you know. A family. They were teeming to take a crack at you, and they didn't care that you were royalty. But you never heard a peep. And Ruby. She betrayed you by working with your uncle. She tried to have you killed by siccing Micah on you. She wanted you out of the way. Did I let that stand? No. I didn't."

I didn't know what to say. I didn't want to say thank you for those things. I didn't want anyone dead for me. Not Enzo. Not Micah's cronies. Not Ruby. Judged, yes. Dead? No. And how long had he been doing this? Decades? A shudder of fear nearly wracked my whole body, but I managed to suppress it.

A change of subject was in order.

"You know so much about me, but I'm at a disadvantage. What's your name?"

His eyes brightened as if he delighted at being asked. "My name is Elias Flynn. You should know the Flynns, but you probably don't. We used to be a prestigious family until your mother had the lion's share of us executed."

I'd known he was probably an Arcadios witch... the

thought trailed off into nothingness as something snapped in my brain. The smell of sea salt surrounded me in a miasma of memory. This was the man I'd danced with at the presentation. He was also in the hallway when the Keys carted Alistair and I off to the holding cells. He had a position of authority, too. Almost like he led them.

This man, Elias, was a Key. He had access to the High Courtroom. He had access to everything. I wondered how many of Caim's records he'd pilfered, how much he knew.

Barrett, I think I found your leak.

"Yes, I just learned of what happened. It must have been awful." My tone was pacifying, but it didn't work—my words only angering him.

"Awful?" He seethed. "Entire families were executed. Women, children. Men. Some of the women were pregnant, did you know that?" His smile was bitter as he began pacing in a short back and forth, even though he had a ton of room.

I had to keep him talking. If he kept talking, he wouldn't do whatever awful thing he had planned. It would give Alistair and the others time to find me—if they even could. Something wasn't right with my magic. Everything felt off—more than it had when I'd gotten slammed with backlash before.

"How did you escape?"

"I was an infant when the Keys raided our home. I wasn't more than a few days old. A Key wanted to kill me but couldn't. He took me under his wing instead, kept me as a son. Told me the story of my family when I was a teenager—with pride, like killing women and children was something to be revered. He didn't survive much longer after that. A dangerous job—being a Key."

Meaning he killed the man who refused to murder an infant. Elias was nearly as old as I was, and he'd been killing since he was a teenager. Nearly four centuries worth of bloodshed.

Empathy, Max, you know that emotion you rarely have? Time to blow the cobwebs off because this man is a bucketful of batshit.

"I can't imagine what you've suffered. I'm so sorry your family was taken from you. But why take my sister? Why summon me here? Why do all those things for me? Maria was a child when the Keys disbanded the coven, and me? I was burned at the stake. Neither of us had anything to do with your family being taken from you."

I'd thought the glint in his eye before was made of malice. Nope. That was a pleasant little preview. The new light in Elias' eyes was made from the very depths of Hell.

"You don't understand anything at all, do you? All

you care about is you. All you care about is getting your sister back. Where is my 'thank you'? Where is my recognition? All these gifts you've been given, and you don't even have the good sense to express the slightest bit of gratitude."

Gratitude? He wanted gratitude for murdering people on my behalf. He wanted a "thank you" for killing an angel in probably the most brutal way possible. He wanted me to be thankful. He wanted me to lick his boots in gratitude.

No. *Hell,* no.

"Maybe because I didn't ask for those things. I didn't *want* Enzo to die. I didn't *want* Micah's friends to die. I didn't *want* Ruby to die. I would *never* ask for those things."

Elias' face fell, hurt staining the almost childlike quality to his pitiful brown eyes. Something was broken in him—even more than I'd previously thought. He assumed I would want these things. Why?

"Why would you think I wanted these actions, Elias?" My tone was soft, not pleading, but like a kind mother who wanted her child to answer a hard question. "Something made you think this. What was it?"

"I watched you, you know? The way you took revenge on the husband of your friend. You killed him. You've killed dozens of evil men and women in your life. You righted wrongs done to other people, but never yourself. You never got revenge on those who did you wrong. You deserved to have your revenge, too."

He began pacing again, but he never moved closer, never widened his track.

"I didn't get revenge on Enzo because there was nothing to get revenge for. He wasn't in the wrong, I was. I lied to him about who I was. When he left me, I knew I'd deserved it. I didn't get revenge on Micah's friends because they didn't kill Melody. And I didn't kill Ruby because she'd been a pawn in my uncle's games. It took me a long time to realize it, but Ruby didn't deserve to die. Get sent to prison for the rest of her life? Maybe. But not die, Elias."

His face twisted, rage painting his expression in slashes of red as he raised his arms up toward the full moon, dead center at the highest point in the sky. It was midnight-ish on the first day of the full moon. I had a feeling Elias was a moon witch. *Shit*.

"You don't like my gifts? You don't appreciate the sacrifices I've made for you? Fine. Then I guess I'll keep your sister. Since you don't like my presents."

The circle surrounding Maria flashed red, but it wasn't the only one.

No, what I hadn't realized, not until this very

moment, was that there were three circles: one around Elias, one empty, and one around me.

And Maria was at the center of them all.

He never planned on letting her go. Because at the center of three circles always lays one thing.

The sacrifice.

CHAPTER TWENTY-FOUR

Have you ever done something so stupid the "after" you was stuck trying to figure out where the hell the "before" you went wrong? This was one of those times. The trouble was, I didn't know how I could have done things any differently.

I had to come alone—I didn't even know where to go until I decided to do this by myself. It wasn't so much as a location, more like a beacon in my mind. I still didn't know where I was, and I was pretty sure Elias weaved the spell to conceal his location just like he weaved a spell to hide his deeds from the Fates. And leaving Maria on her own just wasn't an option. I had a feeling this was all some massive catch-22. I was going to be screwed either way—at least this way I *might* have an option to save my sister.

But "might" was the operative word. Because I was stuck inside a three-ring circle made up of charged moonstones and salt, which meant it was a Venn diagram of awful. Not to mention, Elias was likely channeling the Arcadios amulet with Ruby's power and who knew who else. I had serious doubts Ruby was the only one he'd drained.

"You were never going to let her go, were you?" I asked, trying to break his concentration enough to stall him. I needed more time. I needed Alistair to come get me. I needed my mom.

"Well," he smiled, the quirky upturn of his lips almost boyish, "I may have fibbed a little. See, here's the thing about the spell I need to do, it requires a witch. A sacrifice, if you will. It's a trade, really. The demon I'm summoning, well, she's going to help me drain your power, and in exchange, this demon needs a body. She's incorporeal, a demonic whisper on the wind, and she wants to be solid again. And your sister, she will provide."

If I had anything left in my stomach, I would've lost it then. He wanted to kill Maria like the Arcadios witches did to those children. He wanted to stuff some demon in her body. All so he could drain me.

"But why do you need the demon? If it means my sister's life, you know I would gladly give my power to you. If you've been watching me all this time, if you know me as much as you say you do, you know this for certain."

I held back the wet that hit my eyes as I pleaded with him, the wet that wouldn't stay contained as he freely crossed from his circle toward my sister's.

"While you make a fine offer, I don't think it will work out too well for me." He lifted an iron spike from the quartz altar.

I knew those spikes very well. Those spikes—the same ones that the Gorgons used to avenge their sister Medusa, the same kind—if not the very same ones—that speared Ruby in her final moments.

"Why?" Hot tears scalded my cheeks as I watched him pick up a hammer.

Avarice crossed his expression before he squashed it. "Teresa Alcado murdered my whole family by turning us in to the Council. It has been my life's work to bring them asunder, the same as her. And after I kill one daughter and bring the other beneath my boot, I'll work on making sure she knows it was me who destroyed her. Soon, it will be her family who is gone."

He would punish us for something we had no part in,

just to satisfy his lust for revenge. Teresa's actions had screwed me over once again.

Figures.

I staggered to my feet, pain lancing every bone and every muscle. I couldn't get through the ward to Maria, but maybe I could get out of the circle that held me, and overload them all somehow. And maybe if I did that, the backlash would go to him since he was the caster and not me. I really hoped it wasn't me.

Sucking in a breath, I tried the only thing I could think of. I drew the athame that had been with me since the beginning, and I sliced the flesh of my hand. The same way I had to overload Alistair's circle, I tried dripping my blood on the moonstones and salt. But as much as I squeezed the droplets from my fingers, the blood refused to land on the barrier.

My blood couldn't get out. If my blood couldn't get out, then neither could I. I tried snapping, which only had me popping out and popping back in again.

Elias laughed at my efforts as he spun the spike in his hand. "I've been watching you for a long time, Maxima. I know all your tricks."

"If you know me so well, you should know I hate that fucking name. It's Max, shithead."

He chuckled once again at my complaint, kind of like

how a father would look at a spirited child. "Oh, I know. I just really enjoy watching your eye twitch when I say it. Now, what do you think? Should I wake Maria up before I ram this spike into her flesh, or keep her asleep?"

I didn't want Maria awake for this. I didn't want to see her face when they pierced her skin. I didn't want those same screams to come out of her mouth that Ruby no doubt screamed.

"You don't have an ounce of mercy in you, do you?"

Elias' eyes danced as he shook his head, a smile stretching his lips wide.

The Keys had been searching for those spikes for centuries, but none were found. And yet, Ruby was murdered with them? I didn't think so. The Keys were dirty. Just like Elias.

"You're a Key, right? Are you their leader?"

Elias spun the spike in his hand again, pondering if he would answer me. "You mean, am I the Sentinel? I was wondering if you were ever going to ask me that."

"You seemed like a big shot when you hauled me to the holding cell. I bet you have a bunch of Keys as your acolytes, don't you?"

He frowned and stopped spinning the sharp spike. "I wiped your memory. You shouldn't remember me in the holding cell."

"I shouldn't remember you dancing with me at my presentation either, but here we are. Memory spells only work for so long on me, even in this circle. But I want an answer to my question. You have a bunch of them doing your bidding, don't you?"

Rage tinted his expression before he wiped it clean.

"Aww, come on, Elias. You've been planning this for the better part of four centuries. You had to have friends. Plus, the fact that the Keys swarmed us in that corridor when no one else knew we were there, well, it's telling, isn't it?"

Elias appeared almost pleased that I'd figured it out.

"You're right. I do have friends." Then he put two fingers in his mouth and whistled. As one, at least twenty men stepped to the tree line, each of them in the same dove-gray suit, and each holding an athame similar to mine. An Arcadios athame.

"Did you know that they only killed members of the Arcadios coven in *Virginia* in 1642? They did nothing to the members still in Spain. But that's the difference between the European Council and the American one. While the Flynn line ends with me, there were several lines that were much more fortunate. Each of them will relish this revenge the same as me. And when our vengeance on Teresa is done? Then we'll go after the Council."

Shit. Even if I could manage to get out of this circle, I couldn't take on twenty men. Not as drained as I was.

"Plus, I have one more friend. You should know her…" He trailed off as he tipped his chin to the western portion of the wood. That's when I watched Bernadette —her aging beauty mask in place—walk from the tree line, stopping just outside the circle.

At first, all I felt was relief. Backup had arrived. But the longer she stood there doing nothing as Elias readied himself for the ritual, I realized she had no intention of helping me. Her gaze was dispassionate as she looked me over, and the betrayal stung worse than if she'd cut me with the blade in her hand.

It wasn't like when we were in the courtroom. She didn't whisper in my head. She didn't change her expression. I'd killed Samael, and this was my punishment. I killed her son, and this was my comeuppance.

Thunder cracked overhead, and this time, I knew it wasn't me even though I wished it was.

I wasn't getting out of this circle. And the longer it took Alistair to reach me, the more I realized neither was Maria.

Not unless I quit this pity party and got my shit together. So what if Bernadette was a bad guy? So what if help wasn't coming? I'd done more with less and still kept right on kicking.

Kneeling, the cool, wet soil dampened the knees of my jeans as I tunneled my fingers into the dirt. I wasn't an earth witch or a moon witch, but both settled my soul. I didn't use anything but myself. And weak or no, I was still stronger than any other witch. I could get out of this. They hadn't made a ward yet that could keep me out, all I needed to do was pluck the strings. And if that didn't work, there were a hundred other things I could try.

Elias Flynn wasn't going to beat me. Not today, and not any other day, either.

I focused my sight on the circle containing me. Moonstones and salt at the base, but a web of tracery light formed a dome of magic around me, the red network of a complicated spell penned me in. It would take some work, but I could do it. If I could touch it. But maybe I wouldn't need to physically touch the ward to unravel it. I could maybe pluck the threads from here.

I concentrated on the first thread, using all my mental weight, I unraveled it bit by bit. Sweat snaked down my brow as I focused on that one thread.

Lightning flashed through the sky, a storm threatening to roll over the full moon. *If only*. Any help Mother Nature could send my way would be appreciated. A moon witch needed the moon to shine if he wanted to do a spell.

Once the first thread was undone, I focused on the second.

"Oh, Maxima," Elias called. "I wonder. Can you unravel my spell before your sister bleeds out?"

My concentration broken, I whipped my head up to watch Elias lift the sleep spell off of Maria. In the next second, the first spike was rammed into the delicate flesh of her right wrist, nailing it to the quartz altar at her side.

Her scream was louder than the thunder and tore at everything I was or ever would be.

In the next second, the other spike was in her left wrist, and even though both her hands were immobile, she writhed on the stone. Begging for help, begging for it all to stop.

"Ria!" I screamed, trying to let her know she wasn't alone. "I'm coming for you, baby sister. I'm coming."

Her screams spurred me on, as I tried to pluck the strings from this stupid ward. The second, third, and fourth unraveled, and I was working on the fifth when Elias produced a third spike. Maria kicked, and spat and fought, but he still caught her feet and hammered them into the stone, pinning her in earnest to the quartz altar.

Elias began to chant, the Latin words floating on the air as he yelled them at the sky. And then I knew without a doubt I wasn't going to break his ward.

I wasn't going to do anything but writhe on the ground as he began to syphon everything that I was from me.

CHAPTER TWENTY-FIVE

My screams rivaled Maria's as the power I was born with felt like it was being ripped from my very bones. I tried to focus on her. Tried to catch Maria's eyes. I wanted her to know she wasn't alone. It was stupid, really, but I'd died a hundred times.

She hadn't.

And unlike me, she wouldn't come back in a few hours or days. If Maria died, that was it. And if she died as a sacrifice, I didn't know if her soul would be gone as well or if it would be stuck, trapped in her body for a demon to feast on forever. Knowing what I knew about the other planes of existence, death didn't affect me like it did humans. I knew where souls went, I knew most of them—the ones who were sent on—would be reborn. On and on until the world ended, the same souls living hundreds of lives.

But loss touched me just like everyone else. And I didn't want to endure losing Maria. Not when I'd just gotten her back.

Bright red blood coated the pale stone, rivulets skating down the quartz to pool at the earth below, but the blood didn't stay there. No, it seemed like it was cycling back into the ground and up through the center of the stone, staining the opaque quartz red.

Movement caught my eye, and I tore my gaze from Maria to the empty circle. It was no longer empty at all. Black smoke swirled at the center, growing larger and larger, filling the dome like a macabre snow globe. Electricity crackled inside the dome, spikes of lightning from within struck the inside of the dome as if the summoned demon wanted out. I supposed it did. But if I had my history right, it was too soon to let the demon free. Maria was still alive, and Elias needed all her blood drained and her heart stopped if his spell was to work.

The agony of Elias' spell had almost abated, and I wondered if that meant I was going into shock. Honestly, shock would be welcome right about now. Then as one, the Keys began to chant, their words matching their leader, and I quickly realized the pain that I thought was agony was nothing in the face of this. This was being peeled alive, this was millions of fire ants devouring my flesh. This was worse than being burned at the stake, or drowned, or any other death I'd suffered.

I couldn't even scream, and I kind of wished that shock would come back because that was way better than this. I'd assumed being drained of power was kind of like being tired. Boy, was I wrong. Being drained was like someone decided they needed to shatter all my bones before fishing the shards from my body one by one.

And the fool I was, I looked at Bernadette, mentally willing her to help me. Wanting her to give a shit about either of us. But she did not do one single thing to help. In fact, she wasn't even looking at me anymore. She was staring off in the distance, as dispassionate as ever. If she would have stared at her nails and yawned, I wouldn't have been surprised.

I quit looking at her and focused on Maria. Her screams had stopped, and her blood coated the quartz altar like a curtain. She'd quit writhing, and I couldn't help but think that was a bad thing. I wanted her to fight. I wanted her to spit and scream. I didn't want her to give up.

If she was going to give up, then it had to be up to

me. I sucked in a breath, and focused on the webbing above me, plucking the strands until I had no power left.

Out. I needed out.

A few threads came loose, but all too soon, I couldn't pull at them anymore. My entire body felt filled with lead, which would be awesome if that lead didn't feel like it was also on fire.

My power lay outside myself, and it called to me like a beacon—the same way Elias called to me when he spelled that parchment. Then it dawned on me. If I couldn't get out, maybe I could get someone in.

I focused on Elias as he chanted the stupid Latin words that stole my power. I focused on his hair, on his eyes, on his face. I focused on him like I'd focused on Alistair while I was drawing that salt circle in my basement. I imagined my fist burying itself in his face. I pictured his jaw breaking, blood pouring from his mouth, his teeth cracking with the force of the blow. I wanted him closer, in this circle with me. Wanted him away from Maria and close enough to reach.

Groaning, I struggled to my hands and knees as the flames of agony licked at my bones. I needed a circle. I needed to command him here. Digging the Arcadios athame in the dirt, I tore a trench in the forest floor, a three foot in diameter circle just big enough for one man. Then I ripped the filthy athame through the flesh of my hand one more time, letting the blood flow in the trench.

Green fire sprung up from the bloody furrow in the dirt as wind thrashed inside the dome of magic I was under. A tornado of soil and bracken whipped through my tiny little environment, rebounding off the magic before swirling some more. I staggered to standing, the world around me swimming. Storm clouds filled the dome as bolts of lightning struck the ground by my feet.

And just like I had with Alistair, I got my wish. Elias' scream as he appeared in my circle was as satisfactory as one would think a trapped enemy would be. This time, I had no intention of overloading the ward that held him in place. I had no intention of him leaving it at all. Shaking, I let my hand trace the boundary of the trap, allowing the power of it to warm my rapidly chilling body.

Only then did I reach inside the circle and latch onto Elias' wrist.

"You have something of mine," I growled through gritted teeth.

I could feel my power roiling under his skin, wanting out, and I obliged, drawing back what was mine. The electric heat of it filled me—nothing like when he was taking it. No, this felt like a warm blanket on a cold day, like hot cocoa, and fuzzy socks. It was the sun on my face and sand in my hair. I could breathe again, and I relished the relief for one moment before I split my focus to the bonds of the circle, snapping strings as if my mind was a sword.

But Elias wasn't going to let his master plan go to shit without a fight. He yanked, and all but tried to pry my fingers from his flesh. Screaming intelligible gibberish, he spat at the barrier between our faces, only to have it hit nothing. He flailed as he reached behind his back, producing a spike hidden in his belt. He slashed with the edged spike, the sharp blade of it ripping into my flesh.

Only then did I let him go. I had enough power back to fight. Leaving him in his prison inside my circle, I stepped through the sparking ward and into a melee.

The Keys were no longer chanting the words that would take my sister from me. No, they were a little too busy with my backup that had finally arrived. Teresa hurled balls of electric fire at a particularly large Key, lighting his dove-gray suit ablaze. Striker in all his phased glory, knocked into a Key with one of his wings, hurtling him toward Andras who suffocated him with his tar-black smoke. Della let out a screech of fury as she lunged for another Key, her fangs burying themselves in his throat as she ripped his flesh. Aidan smoked behind a Key, cutting through his neck with his blade before smoking out to find the next. A Key stumbled at my feet, scrambling away from a blackened and flaming Alistair. The burning runes etched into his flesh glowed in the night as he stalked toward his quarry, only pausing to flash me a smile before he continued on his quest for blood.

"Where's Bernadette?" I asked before he got too involved in the killing.

Alistair didn't answer me, he simply pointed to the circle that contained the smoke demon with his flaming sword—*not a euphemism at all, I swear*. I searched for Bernadette in the smoke —the woman that was probably the biggest threat of them all—but what I saw surprised me. She wasn't in her aging beauty costume. No, she was in her real form—the form of a young woman named Lilith. And Lilith was screaming at the top of her lungs, an unholy shriek that seemed to disrupt the smoke.

So, she was helping?

I'd need to talk to my grandmother about which side she was really on later. I had better things to do, like getting Maria out of here. From the outside, it was much easier to disrupt the circles—especially with an Arcadios blade in my hand. The dagger cut through Elias' circle like butter. I was about to cut through the demon's circle when a gray-suit-wearing Key tackled me.

We rolled in the dirt, me losing my athame when I fell. But that athame wasn't my only weapon. Gritting my teeth against the pain in my hand, I snapped both fingers and watched as his neck snapped, nearly twisting the head completely off his body. I noticed a circle of bronze at his ruined throat, the amulet of an Arcadios witch. Those amulets likely had more power than anyone knew what to do with, and I wondered how many souls were trapped in those little circles of metal.

Ripping it from him, I crushed the bronze in my fingers until it was dust. A wisp of glowing white trailed from the dust in my palm, crackling and fizzling into nothingness.

Elias screamed as the soul was ripped free, making me think all the amulets were tied to him somehow—like he was drawing power from more than just his. He was drawing from them all.

"Destroy the Arcadios amulets!" I made my way around Teresa burning a Key alive with her mind, and Andras ripping limbs off another. Gross. My parents were so fucking gross.

I needed to get Maria the hell out of here. I ripped through the demon's circle, caring a little that it might fuck with Bernadette's attack. But I should have known better than to worry, the smoke writhed at her feet as if in pain.

I shattered the rest of the circle that used to hold me. My last barrier gone, I sprinted for my sister. Maria's breath was shallow, the blood running from her wounds slowed to a trickle. Her eyes were open, though, and she stared off at the moon above us as she struggled to swallow.

Wetness hit my eyes, and for once, I didn't hold it back. I let the hot tears rush down my face as I wrapped my hands around the spike in her feet.

"I'm so sorry, baby girl," I whispered and then yanked, pulling the edged spike from her. I did it two more times to the ones at her wrists, and all the while she didn't so much as whimper.

Her breath stuttered, stalled, and then stopped.

Somehow, my hands found their way to her chest as I kept her heart beating with compressions.

"You don't get to leave me, little sister. Do you hear me?" I shouted, counting the compressions in my head. "I just got you back, and I'll be damned if you're leaving me again."

The green liquid fire of my magic glowed at my fingers as they interlaced at her sternum, pressing again and again in the rhythm of her heartbeat. I forced my magic into her, willed it to close her wounds and keep her heart beating, forced the power I didn't understand to keep my baby sister alive.

Then she took a breath on her own, and I couldn't stop myself from tugging her off that fucking quartz rock and hugging her. I also may have peppered kisses all over her face, which I hadn't done since she was a toddler, but if that was wrong, I really didn't give a fuck. My only wish was for her to open her eyes. I wanted to see those beautiful browns full of mischief. I wanted to see them sparkle, but mostly, I just wanted to see them open.

"*Aidan*," I shouted, searching around for the wraith I hadn't spoken to in half a year except to toss against a wall. I was going to have to apologize for that. Maybe. Later, though.

He smoked in right next to me, kneeling in the dirt. I wanted to look him in the eye, but I couldn't peel my gaze from Maria.

"Can you take her to Ian? I don't know how long my magic is going to work, and she needs blood and whatever other juju he can do to keep her alive. Can you do that for me?"

He pressed a hand to his chest. "I'd be honored," he whispered and gathered my sister in his arms, whisking her off to wherever his brother was.

With my main purpose gone, I felt almost lost until I caught sight of Elias trying to break out of his prison, slashing at the ward with the spike that could kill demigods. Funnily enough, it didn't make a dent in my magic. Interesting…

Elias screamed obscenities and promises of vengeance, and all I wanted to do was kill him. I wanted to snuff him out like he nearly did to Maria. The Fates hadn't specified if they wanted him dead or alive, now did they?

But I needed proof that it wasn't Alistair or I that killed Ruby. I needed him to confess all his misdeeds, unearth all of his dirt, and name every single one of his cohorts. Then, and only then, would I make sure he left this earth. Maybe I'd let Alistair escort him personally to the Arcadios wing.

But first, he needed to be neutralized.

Clenching my fists, I let my power go, enjoying his scream a little too much when lightning bolts speared him over and over. Elias crumpled in the dirt long enough for me to snatch the spike from his lax fingers with one hand and the Arcadios amulet with the other. I passed off the spike to Alistair and drew my athame. Only then did I slice through the circle, and this time, there was no blowback.

Sheathing the blade, I pressed my fingertips into his sternum, making sure my pinky and thumb were spread wide. Wind whipped at my hair and thunder cracked close to us, but I didn't worry. I'd done this twice already, hadn't I?

The ground quaked beneath my feet as I turned my hand to the right, and I gleefully watched as the red aura of Elias' magic that had been hidden when we met, sputtered and died.

CHAPTER TWENTY-SIX

Watching Elias' bloody face slide across the marble on the same floor where he murdered Ruby seemed just desserts to me. He would be lucky if I didn't spike his ass there, too, but he didn't move, the sleep spell I put on him keeping him down easily enough. The Fates stood at the wide steps of the dais, watching me with a peculiar expression on each of their faces. It was a little bit of proud threaded with a heavy dose of disbelief.

They didn't think I could do it. *Pfft. Rookies.*

I snapped my fingers, producing a chair for myself and gleefully dumped my tired bones onto the green velvet. Another snap provided the matching ottoman, and as soon as I placed my feet just so, I relaxed for maybe the first time since before I started getting ready to meet the three sisters in the first place.

"You want us to believe the Sentinel is the perpetrator in Ruby's death?" Atropos sneered.

Did that woman have any other expression?

"Well, since I ripped an amulet off his neck with the Arcadios emblem on it, and it likely contains Ruby's soul, and he tried to put an incorporeal demon inside my sister while draining my power for his own ends, well, *yeah*. I kinda do. But if you don't believe me, you can ask any one of the witnesses I have provided." I gestured to the mass of Ethereals behind me.

Teresa, Andras, Bernadette, Della, Striker, Aidan, and Alistair all stood in a line behind me. Bloody, dirty, and tired, the eight of us faced off against the three Fates and the rest of the Council. Barrett was fit to be tied, and Marcus was having a tough time calming him down. It seemed that Elias' specialty was cloaking and memory spells. I wasn't the only one who had been duped by the Arcadios moon witch, I was just the first one to break through his workings.

After I turned off Elias' power like a faucet, all of his spells had been broken. Every memory spell, every cloaking spell, everything. And without his amulet that housed I didn't know how many souls, he was no longer out of the Fates purview.

"And the eight of you decided it was within your right to exterminate the Keys in league with him?"

"Considering they were trying to kill us. Yep." I popped the "p" so they knew without a doubt I did not give a single fuck if they didn't like my methods. "You said, and I quote, 'We want you to resolve all of this. Immediately. You have forty-eight hours to bring the killer to us.' You said nothing about not killing anyone. You don't like my methods? Give me more than two days and fuck all to go on, and maybe you'd get a more conservative outcome. I did the best with what I had. And I'm not sorry. Every single one of those men had an Arcadios amulet with one or more souls inside. They were evil men. I did you a favor. You're welcome."

What I really wanted to know was—where the hell were they when all this bad shit was going down? Where were they when a phoenix leader was committing mass genocide? Where were they when Iva was stealing the souls of the aegis, or when Baron and Bella were trying to break their mother out of Hell? Where were they when Samael was trying to stage a coup, or Micah was trafficking humans? Where the fuck were they?

One angel was killed, and now they care? I wanted to call bullshit, but I didn't. All I did was sit there and give them my best bitch face.

"You don't like the way we do things?" Lachesis asked, but it was more like a statement.

I could feel the sneer on my face when I answered: "*You think?*"

She continued on as if I didn't say anything, "You don't understand that we cannot interfere more than we already do. We provide visions to seers and oracles—we request tasks from some of our retinue. That is all we are allowed to intervene. The consequences are more than any of us could pay if we step out of line. So, when you think we sit on our hands and do nothing, I suppose you are right, but it is because we have been chained that way. Not because we desire to do nothing. It is just that nothing can be done."

I narrowed my eyes at the three sisters, studying them. Clotho seemed the nicest, Lachesis appeared the most apathetic, and Atropos was the angry one. But Clotho was only nice because everyone loved her. She made life, so everyone was on her side. Lachesis was the most ignored, so she ignored the world, and Atropos was pissed off because everyone feared her.

None of them chose their roles—of that I had no doubt—and yet they had the part they had to play.

I nodded to Lachesis and averted my gaze to Atropos. "I understand. We're all doing what we can, right? While you're evaluating what you can and can't do, a 'please' every once in a while wouldn't kill you. Not every job should be done out of sheer spite."

"I'll take it under advisement, and we'll discuss it at the next staff meeting." Atropos' smile was pure "fuck you." Meaning she would look into not being a royal bitch sometime between "never" and "go fuck yourself."

Fair enough.

"You do that, and while you're at it, maybe don't try and blame me or anyone else for shit you know we didn't do. Make no mistake, that isn't a request. You can make of that what you will, but I won't stand for that tactic again. Am I clear?"

Clotho put a hand on Atropos' shoulder, probably calming the Fate before she lost her mind at my challenge.

"You are honorable, that we understand. We also understand that it has been a lifelong mission of yours to protect the innocent." Clotho shifted her feet before stepping down from the dais so we were on equal ground. "You accepted the demon seat on the Council, but the three of us feel you might be suited for another position—one that appeals to your need to right wrongs. If Ruby taught us anything, it taught us that we have an internal problem. Samael, Ruby, Elias, the Keys… evil has somehow infiltrated our ranks. We need you to snuff it out."

Baffled didn't even come close to what I was feeling. "You want me to step down from the Council—a job I finally decided on a few days ago—to what? Fix your problem?"

"If you stay on the Council, it will be your problem, too. But if you take the mantel of Sentinel, you will be in a better position to make real change and stomp out the threat that poses to topple us from within."

I considered her proposal. Me, as some kind of supernatural narc? I couldn't see me doing anything like that. But if it meant being on the ground, if it meant helping people who needed it, then it couldn't be worse than the Council—even if I didn't exactly get a real shot of actually sitting in the seat.

"Would I have to wear the dumb gray suit?" I quirked a brow, and only Striker, Aidan, and Alistair snickered at my sort of joke.

"No. There isn't a uniform," Clotho answered.

"And who do I work for?"

Clotho smiled because she realized I was actually considering it. "You are your own boss. You take requests from the Council and we three, but you can choose what you investigate. We would formally request that you investigate any further Key involvement in the Arcadios mess, but that would be up to you to accept."

"I will take the job on a few conditions."

"What? You want a pony, too?" Atropos flicked her wrist, losing her grip on her attitude.

"While a pony would be nice," I tried to rein in my need to flip her the bird, "I'd want all of you to consider Alistair Quinn for my vacant demon seat. Out of the three remaining candidates, he wants the job, is well versed in demon politics, and isn't a complete dick. Whatever you think you know about him, I want you to accept him into your circle. Because I know honorable men, and he, without a doubt in my mind, is one. He will be a great addition to the Council."

I didn't look at Alistair while I sang his praises, but I felt his eyes on me all the same.

Atropos and Clotho appeared surprised at my request, but Lachesis only gave me a smile and a nod.

"Agreed. If he accepts, he can take your vacant seat. What else?"

I thought about what I would change if I could, and some like-mindedness in the ruling class couldn't hurt. "I want the Council to reach out to the other factions to fill the vacant seats. There is not a sitting phoenix or wraith on the Council, and I believe that this should change."

"I concur." Barrett interjected. "We've been asking for this for years. Now is the time to bring in new blood. Blood we can trust to do the right thing."

This time it was Atropos who agreed. "Fine. If they accept the mantle, then we will have them. Anything else?"

"That's all I have. As long as the job includes ripping every bit of knowledge from Elias before his sorry ass is deported to Hell, count me in."

Atropos' smile was practically gleeful. "Oh, don't worry about that. I think we'd all love to know his secrets, and luckily enough, you have a vampire as one of your paladins. Getting him to talk should be easy as pie."

Paladins? "What do you mean Della is a paladin? And what do you mean by 'one of'?"

Atropos frowned. "You're royalty, Maxima. You've had protection since your Rogue status was lifted. I assumed you knew…"

I shook my head, willing her to keep talking, but it was Bernadette who stepped in between the Fates and me.

"I assigned you protection after Samael was…" She trailed off, her gaze shifting off of me and to someone at my back. "After Samael was judged, I made sure you had protection. I'd put Della in place before, but I added Striker and Aidan as extra protection after you rightfully took my son down. For the past six months, the three of them have been eliminating threats to your life. Della as your close guard, and the boys as your far."

I felt my eye twitching, and when the ground started its rumbling, I took a deep breath to make the earthquakes stop.

"You mean before you stopped talking to me altogether, you enlisted my friends to play bodyguard?"

"Not that I have to explain myself to you, but I needed that distance to infiltrate Elias' inner circle. I used Samael's death as a springboard. I couldn't be chummy with you and keep the façade, so I cut you off. Keep in mind, it was me who called in the backup. Keep in mind, it was me who destroyed one of my own tonight."

"No one is saying what you did wasn't awesome. All I'm saying is a heads up would have been nice. Maybe I wouldn't have been worried that you hated me, if you just would have said something. But that's not your style, is it?"

Glancing over my shoulder, I took a hard look at my bodyguards. "I expected more out of you three. We'll be discussing this at length later."

I stared past my grandmother back to the Fates, the act as much of a dismissal as I could muster. "Knowing now what I do about the Arcadios coven, I understand why you thought displaying that blood would be an affront. But I didn't display Arcadios blood. I displayed my witch side, my mother's blood. Alcado blood."

The three Fates frowned in confusion, but I continued, "I may not be a very good witch or a very good demon, but in presenting myself to you, I wanted to show both sides of me. Because I'm not one or the other. I am both. And maybe you don't like that, but that's who I am, and even though I'm just learning to accept it, I hope you can, too."

Atropos blinked in what I would call shock, but I couldn't be sure. Then she nodded, her head giving me an almost bow. When she rose, she speared my mother with a glare and then turned her gaze back to me.

"I think, Sentinel, what you are is still being discovered."

CHAPTER TWENTY-SEVEN

Soon after Atropos' cryptic pronouncement, we carted Elias off to one of the Key's holding cells. The shifter guard I knew there, Macallan, promised to keep him secure until I needed him for questioning—which would be after at least a full day of sleep and enough food to make my stomach burst. I gave him a way to contact me if any trouble arose, praying he wouldn't need it.

I didn't get a chance to see Alistair once I was done. The Council—which I was no longer a member of—was having a closed-door session. The fact that I was on the outside once again burned a bit, but I tried not to let my insecurities get the best of me.

Teresa, Andras, and Bernadette waited for me outside

the holding area, the trio doing their best not to kill each other. I could tell that the tense détente wouldn't last.

"I'm sorry." The words from Andras caught me by surprise. "I should have gone to you when we got the letter from Elias. We should have included you instead of listening to others when they said you would lose focus. You have always put others ahead of yourself, and we—I—worried that you wouldn't do what I thought you should. I haven't been a father to you ever, but I want to try to not be such a raging asshole."

Okay, who was he, and what did he do with my dick of a dad?

Teresa stepped in front of him as she latched onto my hands. "And I'm sorry I didn't spill about the Arcadios stuff without vamp help. I thought it was behind me, and I wasn't ready to dredge it up. I'm glad you had Della yank it out of me."

My eyes narrowed at the admission. I turned to my grandmother. "Did you dose them with something?"

"This, my dear, is personal growth. They nearly lost you and Maria, and even though I owe you an apology as well, I'll wait a bit. Tea next week once you're rested?"

"You going to spill all the dirt and make sure I'm ready for this Sentinel bullshit?"

Bernadette rolled her eyes in the classy way only she could. "Of course."

"And the Quinn dirt?"

"Now you're just being a pain. Yes, I will spill all the tea while we drink some. Hopefully with some bourbon because I missed you to pieces. Okay?" She held her arms open for a hug.

I gave her a stink face but still hugged the shit out of her. "Quit keeping me in the dark, Grams. It sucks, okay?"

"I'll do better."

Once I breathed Aether-free air again, I pointed my feet toward home, only slightly irritated at the three bodyguards that tagged along. Since the sun was up, I opted for the passenger seat of Striker's obnoxiously overpriced car, nearly falling off my feet as I made my way to Maria.

Déjà vu hit me hard as I walked into the room, nearly the same scene as last year playing before my eyes. Maria in my guest bed—which was now her room—and Ian watching to see if she would wake up. Ian broke up with me in this room, and yet, the sting of it was gone. And Ian didn't look at me like I'd just betrayed him. Now he looked at me like I'd just brought him a gift.

"She wake up at all?"

Ian shook his head and stood, reluctantly releasing Maria's hand. He gestured for us to step out of the room like a good doctor would. But this didn't feel like he was a detached physician giving me news. This felt like he gave a shit, and not about me, but Maria. Good.

"Your spell to keep her heart beating lasted just long enough for me to get a transfusion into her. Physically, she will heal. I don't know what Elias did to her during the hours he had her. I don't know what she endured. She's likely going to need some assistance. I have a contact who helps Ethereals deal with these types of traumas. I can call her. When Maria wakes up."

After the ordeal with Micah, Ian tried to get me to talk to his contact, but I refused. I'd make sure Maria didn't follow my bad example.

"You care a lot about her, don't you?" I asked, not because I was jealous, but because I wanted to make sure what I was about to say came out right if something like this ever could.

"Of course I do."

"I know at one time you thought I was yours—that wraith bonding juju you guys have. But the girl in the club you kissed, she died. In your arms, if I remember right. We didn't work because I didn't trust that you could keep yourself safe. That you wouldn't leave me, that you wouldn't die. And looking back, we also didn't work because you thought the same damn thing about me. We didn't trust each other, and we never would. Not about those things."

Ian huffed and crossed his arms. The burn of him leaving didn't hurt anymore. He wasn't meant for me, maybe he never really was.

"I don't blame you for ending things. If I was honest with myself, I didn't give us even half a chance. But if you aren't pursuing Maria because of me, I will blame you. So, if you have feelings for her, I say go for it. But…" I trailed off, thinking of the exact way to phrase this so my meaning was clear. "If you break her heart? I'll kill you. Cool?"

Ian flashed me that blindingly white smile that I used to love so much. Now, I just liked that my friend was happy. "Cool. Can I go back to my patient now?"

"Yep. I'm going to go eat and then sleep for a week. But if my sister wakes up, I expect you to get me up."

"Will do."

I left the hall and headed for the kitchen, praying there were at least some leftovers in the fridge. Sitting at my kitchen table were the three people I did not want to see.

"I'm too damn tired for your apologies. The first one of you to give me food gets my eternal gratitude and a single freebie pass on being an asshole for not telling me they were assigned to be my bodyguard."

Della held up a greasy white paper bag with the *Mi Cosina* logo on it.

"Sweet mother in heaven, there had better be tamales in that bag," I whispered, the awe in my voice apparent.

Mi Cosina was a restaurant in Texas that had the best tamales on the planet. Someone had to have traveled to Texas to get them, and considering that it was too damn early in the morning, Della had to have compelled a cook to make them. This was a team effort.

"So, what did you bring to say sorry, you shit?" I asked Striker.

In answer, he produced a bottle of bourbon that had to have cost at least five hundred dollars in one hand, and the last Arcadios amulet in the other.

"I stole this," he said, handing over the amulet, "and I bought the bourbon. I kinda figured that you knew better than me what to do with the amulet, and I thought you might want to set her free. I didn't trust what the Fates would do with her, and…"

I felt the bronze in my hand, cold even though it had been in Striker's pocket for hours, and I could almost feel the souls roiling within it. A wave of sadness rolled over me, and I abandoned my guests, leaving them in the kitchen so I could do this part alone. I walked out to the courtyard under the wisteria trees and jasmine vines and spoke to whatever part of Ruby that was left.

"I don't know what made you do what you did. I

don't know if you thought you were doing good or not. I guess it's not up to me to judge. Not anymore. I hope this brings you peace."

Closing my fingers over the circle of metal, I let my power rise in me as I crushed the amulet into dust. I could almost hear a sigh of relief when trails of luminescent smoke rose from my palm, fading off into nothing. And if I shed a tear at the gravity of it, well, that was just me being tired is all.

I dusted off my hands and headed back inside to eat.

I WAS GOING TO MURDER WHOEVER WAS ringing that doorbell. Groaning, I snatched off my covers, ripped the robe off my bathroom door, and stomped to the front door tying the robe closed over my rather inefficient jammies.

What the fuck were bodyguards there for if no one would answer the bloody door?

On my porch was a familiar face, and if I remembered right, I was pretty sure I told him he wasn't allowed back without an invitation. Alistair's paladin, shifted from foot to foot on my doorstep, nerves getting the better of him.

"Ren, I think I told you not to come back unless I asked."

He gave me a hesitant grin. "Yes, Majesty, but Mister Alistair asked me to deliver a present, and since I wanted to apologize for the part I played in your deception, I decided that—"

"You wanted to completely ignore what I told you to do, and do whatever the hell you were going to do anyway? Yeah, I caught that. I remember hearing something about a present? Gimme and then beat it. I need about three days more sleep." I held my hands out for the giant white dress box he had a death grip on.

"Yes, Majesty." He gave me a slight bow, handing over the box.

"Ren, we talked about this 'Majesty' shit. It's Max. Just Max."

"Right. Well, I'm off. I hope you enjoy your present." He turned off my porch as I slammed the door and locked it.

I attacked the cobalt-blue ribbon with a singular focus of a woman opening the first present that likely wasn't a blade of some kind in nearly ten years, with only a minor mental nudge that the ribbon matched my hair to the exact shade. Belly flutters hit me before I lifted the lid. Actual belly flutters.

The lid went bye-bye, and I gently pulled the cobalt paper back. Inside the box laid a set of supple fighting leathers with some kind of magic enhancement. I lifted the moto-style jacket out of the box, and a card fluttered to the floor. Hesitantly, I reached for it, appreciating Alistair's manly, nearly illegible scrawl.

But his words didn't quite make sense.

M—

Looking forward to working with you. I know without a doubt your ass will look fabulous in these. Can't wait to see it.

—Alistair

P.S. I hope to cash in on our deal soon enough.

The deal? Didn't I already pay up when I gave him the demon seat?

But that wasn't what he asked for, was it? He asked for a favor. One of his choosing.

The devil really was in the details.

Max's story will continue with
Sister of Embers & Echoes
Rogue Ethereal Book Four

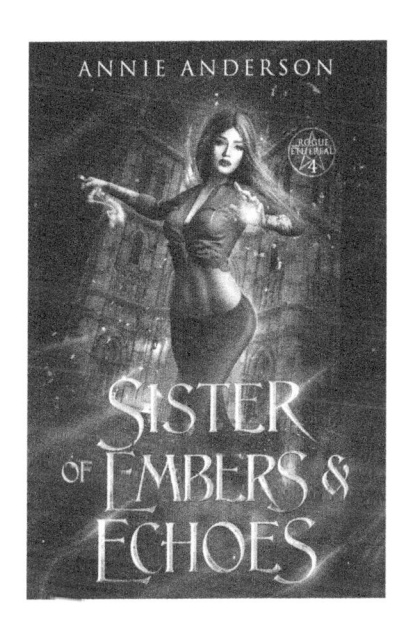

SISTER OF EMBERS & ECHOES
Rogue Ethereal Book Four

Demons, murder, and a trip straight to Hell...

I thought I'd get a little time off before the veritable poop hit the fan, but fate — or rather the Fates — have other ideas. The witch who tried to have my sister possessed has escaped, and not only do I find him dead, but I don't have a clue who he was working with. Or working for...

Now I have a Council Member in human jail, a ragtag

bunch of stuffy law-abiders to lead, and a solid inkling that the next person on the chopping block is me.

All of that would be bad enough, but I've got bigger problems. Maria isn't quite right after a demon almost stole her body, and I have a hunch it's going to require a trip to Hell to get it fixed.

Time to sharpen my athames. Vacation time is over.

Grab Sister of Embers & Echoes Today!

THE PHOENIX RISING SERIES

an adult paranormal romance series by Annie Anderson

Heaven, Hell, and everything in between. Fall into the realm of Phoenixes and Wraiths who guard the gates of the beyond. That is, if they can survive that long…

Living forever isn't all it's cracked up to be.

Check out the Phoenix Rising Series today!

THE SHELTER ME SERIES

a Romantic Suspense series by Annie Anderson

*A girl on the run. A small town with a big secret.
Some sanctuaries aren't as safe as they appear…*

Planning to escape her controlling boyfriend, Isla's getaway hits a snag when a pair of pink lines show up on a pregnancy test.

Levi just needs an accountant. Someone smart,

dependable, and someone who won't blow town and leave him in the lurch. When a pretty but battered woman falls into his arms, he can't help but offer her the job. If only he can convince her to take it.

As an unexpected death rocks this small Colorado town, Isla can't help but wonder if her past somehow followed her to the one place she's felt at home.

Check out the Shelter Me Series today!

JOIN THE LEGION

EXCLUSIVE SNEAK PEEKS,
GIVEAWAYS, BOOK DISCUSSION.
COME FOR THE BOOKS
STAY FOR THE MEMES.

To stay up to date on all things Annie Anderson, get exclusive access to ARCs & giveaways, and be a member of a fun, positive, drama-free space, join The Legion!

facebook.com/groups/ThePhoenixLegion

ABOUT THE AUTHOR

Annie Anderson is the author of the adult urban fantasy Rogue Ethereal series, its paranormal romance prequel Phoenix Rising series, and the upcoming sassy UF Grave Talker series. As a military wife and United States Air Force veteran, Annie enjoys reading or diving head-first into any art project she can get her hands on. Originally from Texas, she is a southern girl at heart, but has lived all over the US and abroad. As soon as the military stops moving her family around, she'll settle on a state, but for now, she enjoys being a nomad with her husband, daughters, and cantankerous dogs.

To find out more about Annie and her books, visit www.annieande.com

- facebook.com/AuthorAnnieAnderson
- twitter.com/AnnieAnde
- instagram.com/AnnieAnde
- amazon.com/author/annieande
- bookbub.com/authors/annie-anderson
- goodreads.com/AnnieAnde
- pinterest.com/annieande

Made in the USA
Coppell, TX
20 January 2021